HIS PREGNANCY ULTIMATUM

BY

HELEN BIANCHIN

MILLS & BOON®

First published in Great Britain 2004
Large Print edition 2005
Harlequin Mills & Boon Limited,
Eton House, 18-24 Paradise Road,
Richmond, Surrey TW9 1SR

© Helen Bianchin 2004

ISBN 0 263 18539 7

Set in Times Roman 17 on 19 pt.
16-0405-36973

Printed and bound in Great Britain
by Antony Rowe Ltd, Chippenham, Wiltshire

CHAPTER ONE

'MIA!'

A slender form almost identical to her own burst forward the instant Mia emerged into Sydney's airport arrival lounge, and within seconds she was engulfed in an enthusiastic hug.

'Hey,' she protested with a musing laugh. 'It's only been five months.'

A sisterhood of two, no parents since their untimely death a decade before, the girls had been the best of friends for as long as they could remember. Sibling rivalry didn't exist, never had, and each was sure it never would.

Petite in height, sable-brown hair, dark brown eyes, their likeness was such they had on occasion been mistaken for twins.

Yet Alice was the elder by two years, divorced with a nine-year-old son.

Mia caught hold of her sister's arm. 'Let's get out of here.'

It took a while to collect her bag from the carousel, clear the busy terminal and join the flow of traffic heading towards the city.

It was great to be home, although *home* was something of a misnomer, for she no longer had a home as such. During the past few years she'd lived on university campus studying for a pharmacy degree.

Mia rolled her shoulders in a bid to ease the lingering tension from too many sleep-deprived nights leading up to end-of-year exams, the lack of caffeine, and a weariness that had little to do with either one of them.

'So, tell me,' Alice begged. 'What's new?'

Hell. Where did she start? Not at all might be best, she decided, while her sister was negotiating busy inner city traffic. It would take a while to reach the northern suburb of Manly, and the kind of news she had to impart was better told seated at Alice's dining-room table while sharing a pot of tea.

'The exams went okay,' Mia reiterated cautiously, aware she'd said as much via email.

'And?'

'It's good to be back.'

Alice gave her a searching look as the car drew to a halt at a controlled intersection. 'You look pale. Tired,' she elaborated.

Mia offered a faint smile. 'Thanks,' she managed ruefully. 'Just what I needed to hear.'

'Nothing some home-cooked food and a good night's sleep won't cure.' The brisk tone was accompanied by a competent smile.

Alice was the ultimate earth mother, taking pride in producing wholesome hearty meals, home-baked cookies and bread, charity bakes. She sewed, stitched, crocheted, knitted, and took pottery classes. It didn't stop there, for she also took art, sculpted, and set oils on canvas. She served on her son's school committee, ran as president of the parent-teacher association, and excelled in organisation of all things.

Ask Alice was an invisible bandana her sister wore with pride, for *helping* had become a mission in life. It made up for the five years of Alice's marriage during which her husband conditioned her to believe she served little purpose and possessed no self-worth.

Mia took in the familiar sight beyond the windscreen. Old buildings merged with new, dull, well-worn red brick jumbled together with renovated terrace houses, newly lacquered ornamental iron railings vying with broken wood palings. An endearingly eclectic mix that marked inner-city suburbia.

Traffic, as usual, maintained a hectic pace in a never-ending river of vehicles jostling for position in a bid to catch the next set of lights and minimise road time.

City smells, combining aged buildings, fuel fumes, summer heat. Trees with spreading branches bordering a green-grassed park, and, above, a cloudless blue sky.

Mia turned her attention to her sister.

'How's my favourite nephew?'

'Great. Matt is doing well in school, enjoyed a terrific soccer season, and is heavily into tennis for summer,' Alice enthused. 'He's studying piano, guitar, and is a whiz at chess. He began martial arts classes this year.'

Maternal love was unconditional, and Alice believed in the 'busy mind, active body' theory...totally. Fortunately her son was an enthusiastic advocate who viewed each new venture as a conquerable challenge.

'I can't wait to spend time with him.' They shared a mutual affection that dispensed with the generation gap, a love of sports, action movies, books. Pals, she accorded fondly, and hoped the *friendship* part of their relationship would never change.

'He has plans,' Alice warned, and Mia offered a wry smile.

'Uh-huh. I take it para-gliding, bungee-jumping and all other dangerous activities are a definite no-no?'

Alice made a sound that was part sigh, part groan.

'Don't,' she warned. 'Even in jest.'

Traffic was heavy as they crossed the harbour bridge, and only began to ease as they cleared the inner northern suburbs.

There were coves with moored craft, a marina, and heavy greenery hugging the elevated rock-face where luxurious homes perched high sharing magnificent views of the inner harbour and city.

Sun-dappled water, stunning architecture…a place where she'd been born and spent her formative years. Excelled and survived, loved and been betrayed, only to emerge as a strong, determined young woman whose focus became unwavering in pursuit of her goal.

Except for one little blip that had the power to change her life for ever.

Alice's home was situated in a wide tree-lined street, a solid double-brick structure with medium-size rooms her sister redecorated with considerable flair at regular intervals.

Externally it was similar to many houses in the established suburb, but indoors it held an air of homeliness that was both inviting and relaxing.

'Coffee, tea, or something cold?' Alice queried as she preceded Mia down the hallway.

'Tea would be great.' There was only one guest room, which she occupied during university vacations, and she deposited her bag, released her knapsack, then she quickly freshened up before joining her sister in the kitchen.

Aromatic tea steamed from two cups, and there was a selection of home-made cookies set out on a plate.

'We have an hour before I need to go collect Matt from school,' Alice declared, indicating a chair opposite. 'So...out with it.'

She could prevaricate, brush off her sister's intuitive questioning, or at least delay giving an answer until...*when*? Tonight, when Matt was asleep? Tomorrow? There was never going to be a *good* time.

'I'm pregnant.' No lead up, just the basic fact. Yet the very starkness of her announcement caused acute anxiety as to Alice's reaction, for Mia's stance on pre-marital sex was a shared, well-known fact.

Together, they'd laughed about it, exchanged views, pursued the 'fors' and 'againsts', whether saving oneself for the *right* man and marriage didn't belong way back in the previous century! 'What if the sex turns out to be...well, *less* than anticipated? How will you *know* if you have nothing to compare it with?' Alice had teased.

Now, there was a tremendous sense of vulnerability along with the anxiety. Everything she'd believed in, all that she'd held dear in her emotional heart, was laid bare, and open to criticism.

It was bad enough she'd resorted to self-castigation every day...every waking *hour*, since that fateful night.

'Just...*I'm pregnant*? That's it?' Alice demanded, aghast.

Mia closed her eyes, then opened them again. Dear heaven, what was the matter with her? 'I need to fill you in,' she managed ruefully, and caught her sister's intent expression.

'In spades. No detail spared. And it would help to know whether I'm to congratulate, commiserate, console, or rejoice with you.'

Her stomach executed a somersault, then went into free fall. 'Commiserate,' she admitted, and didn't know whether to laugh or cry.

'You weren't—?' Shock and anger meshed with a fighting spirit second to none. 'It wasn't—?'

'*No,*' she reassured at once, her own shock a visible entity. 'Nothing like that.'

Alice leaned forward and covered her sister's hand with her own. 'So—what happened?'

The genuine concern evident in her sister's expression almost moved her to tears, and she shook her head in self-chastisement of the emotional roller coaster she'd been riding for the past few weeks. One minute she'd be fine, the next a teary mess.

Where did she start? *'Who,'* she corrected wryly. Oh, yes, it was definitely *who*.

'I assume he's to die for,' Alice opined with a faintly wicked smile. 'Considering he managed to persuade you to discard every one of your preconceived convictions about sex before marriage?'

His image came sharply into focus, haunting, taunting her with what they'd shared together. The excitement, the ecstasy…and her wantonness to experience it again, and again. A willing pupil beneath a skilled lover's touch, she reflected.

'Incredible,' she said simply, aware of the warmth flooding her cheeks as she held her sister's gaze.

'Off the planet, huh?' Alice's grin was replaced with curiosity and a degree of mild reproof. 'You didn't tell me you were with anyone.'

Alice's surprise was understandable, given they spoke on the phone each week and resorted to email almost every day.

'I'm not.'

Her sister's eyes narrowed fractionally. 'If you don't give me the rundown...the *total* rundown,' she endorsed, 'I'll be forced to take dire action!'

Mia managed a faint smile. 'The short version won't wash?'

'Don't even think about it!'

There was nothing else for it but to start at the beginning...something she should have done at the onset, instead of dropping a verbal bombshell in her sister's lap.

'I was supposed to meet a friend at an evening function.' A night out had seemed a good idea at the time, following weeks of intense study. It had also provided the opportunity to dress up…a marked change from wearing the usual university garb of jeans and tee shirt. 'She didn't show,' Mia went on to explain. 'When I checked my cellphone there was a text message to say she'd become suddenly ill.' She effected a faint shrug. 'I didn't know anyone there, and I was about to leave when I noticed a fellow guest standing alone on the other side of the room.'

A man whose magnetic presence had made the room and everyone in it fade into insignificance.

Even from a distance he'd had an alarming effect on her equilibrium. Disturbing, disruptive, *lethal*. In that instant she'd instinctively known her emotional life was about to go into a tail-spin.

Yet not even she, in her naïvety, could have possibly imagined how the evening would end, or its far-reaching implications.

Nor would she have believed she could fall so quickly, so easily beneath a man's spell.

Not one day passed when she didn't query her sanity in mindlessly giving in to temptation...yet that was a misnomer, for she'd been fully aware of her actions, and honesty demanded acceptance she'd been a willing, eager participant.

'You dated him?'

Oh, hell, this was where it became... difficult. 'Not exactly.'

Alice's expression sharpened. 'What do you mean...*not exactly?*' There was fleeting comprehension, followed by full-blown shock. 'You slept with him that same night?'

There hadn't been much sleep, only sheer physical and emotional exhaustion in the early pre-dawn hours.

'Dear God, Mia.' Her sister's voice reduced to a stunned whisper. 'What were you thinking?'

She closed her eyes against the anguish of her foolishness. 'That's just it. I didn't *think.*'

Her sister's eyes narrowed. 'I take it the sex was consensual?'

'Oh, hell, *yes*.' The man, the night, the sex filled her mind in vivid detail. His powerful image, his touch, everything about him was indelibly imprinted in her mind.

Alice discarded her tea and sank back in her chair. 'You had a wild night with someone you'd never met before?' She shook her head in silent disbelief. 'My sensible sister who's so selective with her body she steadfastly refused to sleep with the man who wanted to put a ring on her finger?'

How could she explain all it had taken was one look, and she'd felt her bones melt? Recognition on some intense instinctive level that went beyond anything she'd ever known before.

'Someone must have spiked your drink.' It was the only logical explanation Alice could summon, and Mia shook her head.

'I wasn't drinking.' There was nothing, no one to blame but herself.

'Have you told him you're pregnant?'

How could she, when she didn't even know his name, let alone where he lived, worked?

Her silence was sufficient answer, and Alice's features softened with distress. 'He's married?'

The thought almost destroyed her. If only for the reason it pegged him as a cheater, and made a bad situation worse. 'I have no idea.'

'Yet you had unprotected sex?' Her sister's face paled at the implications. 'Are you insane?'

'One of the condoms broke.'

Alice's gaze widened. 'One?' She waited a beat. 'Oh, my.'

Oh, my didn't come close. The sex had been mind-blowing, passion at its zenith…for her. Had it been the same for him? He hadn't said, but then neither had she. In truth, she hadn't been capable of uttering a word.

'You don't have his name? Anything?'

It sounded crazy to admit an exchange of names hadn't seemed important at the time. Worse, it hadn't even entered the equation.

'I left while he was still sleeping,' Mia revealed after an agonising silence, not adding her sense of sick shame, or the furtiveness with which she'd donned her clothes and crept from the room, the hotel, and summoned a cab.

Oh, Lord…how could she have discarded every moral she'd held dear all her life for one night with a man she'd never met before? Worse, would undoubtedly never see again?

It didn't make sense any more *now* than it had then. And she couldn't even claim her decision to go with him had been clouded by alcohol.

'Are you considering a termination?'

Pain clenched deep inside, a tangible entity that momentarily clouded her eyes. She wanted this child. So much so, she couldn't bear the thought of extinguishing its foetal life. It was a part of her, *him*. A vivid reminder of what they'd shared. 'Do you think I haven't agonised over that decision every hour of every day?'

'And?'

'I recognise the wisdom associated with termination, given the circumstances,' she offered slowly as she met and held her sister's gaze. 'But I don't think I can do it.' She lifted a hand and smoothed a stray tendril of hair behind her ear, then attempted a faint smile that somehow didn't quite come off.

As close as they were, she couldn't bring herself to admit that what she'd initially damned as unbridled lust was something much deeper, more meaningful than just the slaking of physical need. It touched her heart, her soul, and captivated both on a level she hadn't dreamed possible.

The child she carried represented part of that.

'No verbal warning about bringing a child into the world and raising it as a single mother?'

'I look at Matt and *know* my life would be as nothing without him,' Alice assured quietly. 'He's my light, my laughter, my joy.'

She paused in reflective silence as she chose her words. 'There are a number of working mothers in today's world. I guess I have to say emotionally it would be easier to share things with a supportive partner,' she added. 'Someone who could cut me some slack every now and then. Share the responsibility. However, if you want reassurance single parenthood can work...I have no regrets, not one.'

'I know it.'

Alice's hands reached out and covered her own. 'I'm sure whatever decision you make will be the right one.'

For me? Or the child?

It was something that had kept her awake nights, diminished her ability to study, and with morning sickness beginning to kick in she was forcibly reminded of the need to make a choice...soon.

'If seeing the pregnancy through is an option, you could transfer to a university here and move in with me.'

Tears sprang, clouding her vision, and she blinked to dispense them.

Unconditional love. It was beyond price, and infinitely precious. 'Thanks.'

'But...?'

Alice knew her well. Too well. 'If I take that option, the responsibility is my own.'

'I kind of figured you'd say that.' An absent-minded sip from her cup brought a murmur of disgust. 'I'll make fresh tea.'

Mia checked her watch. 'You don't want to be late collecting Matt.'

Her sister groaned. 'I need to take him on to the tennis club for coaching.'

'We can pick up something to go, and drink it while we watch him.'

They did, and Matt's enthusiastic welcome lightened Mia's heart a little as she applauded his good shots with as much fervour as his mother.

Was this where she'd be in ten years? Cheering her son or daughter on from the sideline? Ensuring there was a host of extracurricular activities to strengthen the mind and body, thus avoiding the pitfalls of vulnerable youth?

The conception of this tiny foetus growing inside her womb was a mistake. Yet its presence existed. If she carried it to term, it would never know its father. And what empathy could she hope to achieve as a mother with her child if she went with honesty and revealed the child's existence was the result of a one-night stand with a stranger?

'Did you see that backhand?'

She had, in an abstracted way. 'Poetry in motion,' she conceded, punching the air for Matt's benefit.

At that moment her cellphone buzzed with an incoming SMS message, and she frowned as she read the text.

'Problem?' Alice queried, and Mia offered a rueful smile.

'Nothing I can't handle.'

Alice's gaze held hers. 'But not one you particularly want to?'

Mia rolled her eyes in an expressive gesture. 'It's—awkward.'

'Explain *awkward*.'

'It's from Cris.'

'One of the students you share lectures with?'

'Yes. His family are Sydney based.'

'That's a problem, *how*?'

'He's nineteen, and he hasn't told his family he's gay.'

Alice's expression didn't change. 'Okay, so why do I get the impression there's more to it than what you're telling me?'

Mia took her time in answering. 'He's a nice guy.'

'And you feel protective of him?'

She summoned a mental image of the tall, lean young man who made her laugh, shared his sharp brain and the benefit of a photographic memory. 'I value his friendship. We share two of the same lectures, and tend to hang out together.'

'There's a preconceived image on campus he's your toy boy?'

'No.' She'd formed friendships with several fellow students and enjoyed their company. Yet she wasn't a *girlie* girl who lived to follow the latest fashion trends, and she veered away from the thinly veiled sexual overtones prevalent in many of the male students.

Cris didn't cause her to put up barriers on any level.

'I've been invited to dinner on Thursday evening.'

'I think you should go,' Alice opined as Matt finished up with his coach and came off the court. 'How difficult can it be?'

Maybe Alice was right. And besides, if she declined on some fabricated excuse the invitation would inevitably be extended to another evening.

SMS made for easy, quick communication, and within minutes it was set, with Cris alerting he'd collect her at six.

'It'll be fun,' Alice assured as they walked to the car.

Mia wasn't so sure. Twice the next day she considered cancelling. Wednesday she made the call, only to cut the connection.

Thursday was way too late, for only an emergency would do...and her patron saint refused to oblige her with one.

Consequently Mia dressed with sophistication in mind. Stiletto heels, the classic black dress, minimum jewellery with the exception of stunning drop ear studs. In the need to complete the image, she swept her hair into a smooth knot and secured it, then teased a few tendrils free to curl below each temple.

'Don't go,' a tiny voice warned as she collected her evening purse and exited the guest room. *Fool*, she admonished. No one would eat her. Besides, she was capable of taking care of herself.

'Looking good.'

Mia offered her nine-year-old nephew an affectionate smile. 'You think?'

'*Wow*, definitely,' Matt declared with a male appreciation beyond his years.

'Your ride has just pulled into the driveway,' Alice forewarned a few seconds ahead of the sound of a car door closing.

Mia rolled her eyes expressively. 'I wish this didn't seem like such a big deal.'

Somehow 'the family would like to meet you' had seemed a light-hearted invitation at the time, but, now it was imminent, she wasn't so sure.

'Cris is a fellow student, a friend. I'm sure his family are very nice.'

The name *Karedes* numbered high among the city's social echelon, and *nice* was debatable, given Cris' version of his family.

Elder brother, Nikolos, who ruled the Karedes Corporation with a fist of steel; their widowed mother Sofia, whose influence was superseded only by Angelena the family matriarch, Nikolos and Cris' widowed paternal grandmother.

The doorbell pealed, and Mia drew in a deep breath as she crossed into the hallway.

'Hi.' Her greeting held genuine warmth for the young man standing in the aperture.

He was attractive, with dark soul-searching eyes, a warm smile and generous heart; his tall frame and lean features held promise of the man he would become.

Introductions were made with ease, and minutes later Mia slid into the passenger seat of a Porsche.

'Yours?' she teased as he sent the car purring down the street.

'It belongs to my brother.'

'And he lets you borrow it?'

'When I'm home.' Cris effected a negligible shrug. 'He has others.'

'As in *plural?*'

'Uh-huh.'

A shiver slid down her spine, for which she had no logical explanation. 'Perhaps you should fill me in on the evening's game plan.'

The Porsche growled to a halt at a traffic intersection, and he spared her a penetrating look. 'You're a friend I happen to regard with affection.'

'Platonic friend,' she conceded, and earned his swift smile.

'That's the description I've offered.'

'Good.'

'They'll adore you. What's not to like?'

Mia offered a slightly rueful smile. There was a part of her that wanted to tell him to turn the car round and take her home.

Get a grip. It was only one evening. A few hours. She'd exchange social pleasantries, decline the obligatory glass of wine and eat fine food.

Rose Bay held an eclectic mix of well-established homes, many with panoramic views of the harbour, and *stately* came to mind as Cris eased the Porsche to a halt out-side a magnificent set of ornate wrought-iron gates guarding entrance to a sweeping driveway that led to a double-level plantation-style home in cream-plastered brick.

Wide bi-fold doors, timbered shutters, pillars and an elegant *porte-cochère*, set in beautiful landscaped grounds, the home… *mansion*, Mia amended…gave hint to serious family wealth. *Very* serious wealth.

Something Cris had neglected to mention.

As if to compound it, a Maybach sat parked beneath the *porte-cochère*. Its opulent lines were easily identifiable as the ultimate in the Mercedes group.

'You're impressed.'

It was a statement, uttered without emotion, and she allowed her gaze to settle on his features. 'Am I meant to be?'

His expression became unreadable as he drew the Porsche to a halt in a designated parking bay. 'It's only stuff,' he said quietly. 'Material possessions gathered and passed from one generation to another as a visual attestation to entrepreneurial success.'

'Which you hate?'

'No. I merely prefer not to hang onto the familial coat-tails.' He reached for his seat belt as Mia undid her own. 'Okay, let's go do this.'

'Face the fray?' she teased lightly, and was rewarded with a teasing smile.

'You got it in one.'

Seconds later they gained the spacious bi-level marble-tiled external entrance, and two large panelled doors swung open to reveal an impeccably attired butler.

'Good evening.'

A *butler*? Why should she be surprised?

Cris executed an introduction. 'Costas has been with the family for years.'

'The family are assembled in the lounge.'

When it came to strict formality, she'd take warm spontaneity any time. Didn't families of Greek origin fall into the latter category?

Perhaps not.

Mia crossed the wide expanse of marble-tiled floor at Cris' side, a few steps behind the butler, who paused on reaching what she presumed to be the lounge.

'Ma'am, your son and his guest are here.'

It was a large, exquisitely furnished room in which two women were seated and a man stood in side profile beside a wall of French doors.

A man whose height and stance struck a familiar chord. One Mia instantly dismissed, despite the swift curl of apprehension twisting her stomach.

The younger of the two women rose to her feet and moved forward.

'Mia. How nice to meet you at last.'

'My mother, Sofia Karedes,' Cris alluded with a smile. 'Mia Fredrickson.'

'Allow me to introduce my mother-in-law.' Sofia indicated the older woman remaining seated. 'Angelena Karedes.'

The matriarch, Mia concluded, meeting Angelena Karedes' intense unwavering gaze. Nothing, she deduced, would pass unnoticed beneath those sharp dark eyes.

'Mia.' It was a polite acknowledgement, nothing more.

'My elder son, Nikolos.'

He turned, and she felt as if her heart suddenly ceased beating.

No. The silent cry rose up from the depths of her soul. It couldn't possibly be...

There had to be a mistake. How could Cris' brother and the man with whom she'd spent a wild night of unbridled sex be one and the same?

Yet his identity was beyond doubt. His height and breadth of shoulder were achingly familiar. So too were his broad-sculpted facial features, the strong jaw, dark eyes, and a mouth that was to die for.

All it took was one look, and her bones began to melt.

Dear heaven...just thinking about what they'd shared almost brought her undone.

He knew. It was there in the depths of his eyes, the sensual curve of his mouth...an in-

stant recognition that appeared fleetingly as
he moved forward to greet her.

She wanted to obey an instinct to turn and
run, and it was only courage that forced her
to remain.

'Mia.'

Her name on his lips sent the blood surg-
ing through her veins, heating her body to
fever pitch, and it was all she could do to
utter a brief acknowledgement.

Did he recognise her discomfort? Worse,
did anyone else in the room sense it?

She wanted to rage against fate for being
so unkind. It was bad enough accepting she'd
discarded every moral she'd held dear for all
of her adult years. Difficult to condone it had
happened with a stranger. Discovering she
was pregnant went right off the Richter scale.

Yet *this*…this was her worst nightmare.

CHAPTER TWO

MIA tried for calm politeness, and held the instinctive feeling she failed miserably.

'Nikolos.' His name on her lips sounded strange, even to her own ears, and she dismissed the inclination to close her eyes, then open them again in the hope she was locked into some nightmarish dream.

In the name of heaven, *get a grip*. In the list of awkward situations, this took top place in her book. But doubtless not in his.

In his late thirties, Nikolos Karedes bore the air of a seasoned sophisticate, well-versed in every social nicety.

Yet she'd caught a glimpse of the man beneath that façade…someone who'd destroyed her previously held defences with galling ease. Worse, she'd allowed him to.

As if she'd had a choice, she reflected wryly, aware of the intervention of a divine power over which she'd had no control.

Had it been the same for him? That instinctive knowledge they were twin halves of a soul? Or was it merely fanciful thinking on her part?

The latter, she perceived with rueful acceptance. Without a doubt.

So her name was *Mia*...Nikolos perceived. The petite sable-haired young woman who'd managed to get beneath his skin in a way no other woman had. The thought, *taste* of her had driven him mad with longing since that unforgettable night they'd spent together twelve weeks ago. She was an itch he couldn't scratch...heat and light and passion, and so much more.

Did she have any idea how he'd felt when he'd woken and found her gone?

Or the steps he'd taken in subsequent days and weeks to try to discover who she was? Each avenue he'd explored had brought no result. It was as if she'd appeared out of no-where, only to disappear.

He'd wanted to wring her neck…dammit, his own, for not anchoring her close to him in sleep so that her slightest move would have brought him awake.

There were occasions when he wondered if he'd dreamed the entire night, *her*…yet he retained a vivid memory of her scent, the clean, fresh smell of her hair, the silky smoothness of her skin beneath his hands, his mouth.

As to her response…the tentative surprise, the burgeoning sensuality beneath his touch, her generosity in giving herself up to him so completely… It had proven a powerful aph-rodisiac that had changed *want* to *need* through the night, and seeded an emotion he hadn't cared to define.

Mia glimpsed the momentary darkness ev-ident in his dark, almost black eyes. The faint edge of mockery, and something else she was unable to determine. Anger? Why *anger,* for heaven's sake?

'Please take a seat.' Sofia indicated a chair close by, and Mia sank into it with a feeling of relief.

'What can we offer you to drink?'

Something strong to settle the wild tango in which her nerves were indulging would be great...except alcohol in any form was a no-no. 'Thank you. A soda,' she indicated. 'Or mineral water.'

Mia was acutely aware of Cris' interested gaze, and that of his grandmother. Sofia seemed intent on acting the gracious hostess. As to Nikolos...his part in this wretched tableau was something at which she could only hazard a guess.

What had held the portent of being a difficult evening had taken a shift for the worse.

How long before she could leave? Two hours, three?

Mia accepted a frosted glass from the proffered tray.

'Cris has spoken very highly of you.'

She could do polite conversation. 'We share a few classes at university.'

'How old are you?' Angelena Karedes demanded, and earned Sofia's chiding protest.

'Please. Mia is a guest.'

Oh, hell, could the evening get any worse? 'Twenty-seven.' She waited a beat. 'Would you like to check my driver's licence?'

The old lady's eyes gleamed. 'Sassy. I like that.' The gaze didn't shift. 'What do you see in my nineteen-year-old grandson?'

Mia's chin tilted slightly. 'A friend.'

'Hmm.'

One word, that wasn't really a word at all, yet it conveyed a wealth of meaning.

'Yiayia,' Nikolos chided gently. 'Enough. You embarrass our guest.'

The matriarch's sharp gaze speared her own. 'Are you embarrassed, child?'

'Do you mean me to be?'

'Dinner is served.'

Costas' announcement was timely, and brought an inward sigh of relief that was short-lived as she found herself seated opposite Nikolos.

Accident or design?

Design, Mia decided. As the eldest male and presumably head of the family, there could be little doubt the reason for his presence was to check out his younger brother's *friend* and deduce an ulterior motive for the friendship.

Familial protectiveness or necessary caution? Undoubtedly both, and, while she could see the sense of it, she abhorred the not-so-subtle interrogation.

Would she have felt differently if Nikolos weren't present, and part of it? Innate honesty compelled an affirmative answer.

He disturbed her...mentally and emotionally. It was almost as if every nerve cell recognised him on a base level, and she had to fight to retain her composure.

Difficult when he was *there*, almost within touching distance on the opposite side of the dining table.

The thought of eating anything made her feel ill, yet good manners ensured she sampled a few morsels from each course...of which there seemed far too many. Or was that merely her imagination, due to her acute sensitivity of the man seated close by?

'Are you a perpetual student,' Angelena queried, 'intent on gaining academic successes without putting theory to practice?'

'If I'd known you would be so intensely interested in my background, I could have brought my CV for your perusal.'

Strike one for Mia, she accorded silently, and heard Cris' appreciative chuckle.

'Are you going to give it up, *Yiayia*?'

His grandmother lifted one eyebrow. 'Have you known me to retreat from anything?' She turned her attention back to Mia. 'What field were you in before choosing to pursue a pharmacy degree?'

For one second she considered going for shock tactics, then opted for fact. 'I was a cosmetics consultant.'

Those shrewd eyes sharpened. 'In a department store?'

'On referral from cosmetic surgeons to teach patients how the skilful use of cosmetics can minimise facial disfigurement.' Exacting work, with often pleasurable results.

'I imagine it was gratifying,' Sofia indicated with interest. 'Did you work with children, or mainly adults?'

'Both.'

Between them they were gradually building up her profile, and she mentally chastised herself for her own cynicism in wondering if it wasn't some preconceived test.

Mia sipped water from her glass, and when it came to dessert she passed on the baklava and settled for fresh fruit.

Another hour, she perceived, then she could plead a need to leave.

'Are you intent on seducing my grandson?'

Now there was a question!

Nikolos fingered the stem of his wine goblet as he waited to see how Mia would handle the elderly lady's irascible manner, intrigued by the slight tilt of her chin, the faint edge of defiance deepening her dark brown eyes.

'No.'

'You are a refreshing change from the simpering socialites who trip over themselves to attract my grandson's attention.'

Costas' appearance was a welcome intrusion. 'Coffee is served in the lounge, ma'am.'

Thank heaven the evening was almost at an end. For the past few hours she'd felt like a specimen beneath a microscope...dissected, analysed, and categorised.

Mia requested tea, and when she finished she stood up, thanked Sofia, Angelena, then she turned towards Cris.

'Would you mind calling me a cab?'

'Don't be ridiculous.' His protest was immediate.

'I'll drive Mia home,' Nikolos inclined smoothly.

A silent scream rose and died in her throat. Oh, dear Lord, *no*. She didn't want to be alone with him. Hell, she didn't want to have anything to do with him!

Except somehow she couldn't dismiss an instinctive feeling he intended to allow her no choice.

'A cab is fine,' she managed evenly, tempering her firm tone with a polite smile.

'No.'

If she thought he'd let her escape so easily, she was badly mistaken. Nikolos leant down and brushed his lips to Angelena's temple, then accorded Sofia a similar gesture of affection.

'Goodnight. I'll be in touch.'

Mia cast Cris a desperate glance, and received a faintly raised eyebrow indicating a silent *What's the fuss?*

If he only knew!

'This isn't necessary,' Mia said quietly minutes later as Nikolos opened the passenger door and stood waiting for her to slip into the front seat.

'You want to cause my mother distress by beginning an argument on her doorstep?'

She flung him a dark glance as she slid into the car, and the door closed with a refined click before he crossed to the driver's side.

The instinct to get out and run was uppermost, and she banked it down.

'I'll accept a ride to the nearest cab-stand,' she indicated stiffly as Nikolos eased the vehicle towards the gated entrance.

'Afraid, Mia?' he posed as the Mercedes gained the leafy avenue and gathered speed.

Sheer bravado was responsible for her answer. 'No.'

'You should be.'

'I don't see why.'

He spared her a brief glance. 'No?' She looked so delightfully petite seated against the opulent leather. 'You'd have me believe what we shared was of little consequence? A one-night stand between two consenting adults?'

Her heart thudded in her chest, then kicked to a faster beat. 'Something like that.'

'The *hell* it was.'

She wanted to hit him, and would have if he hadn't been in control of a car. 'There's a cab-stand at Double Bay. You can drop me there.'

Nikolos' hands tightened on the steering wheel as a knot tightened in his gut. Something primeval stirred deep within in the knowledge he'd been her first and only lover. He tamped down the need that rose so swiftly, and stifled a husky oath in self-castigation.

He was far beyond the ready lust of a teen-ager. Yet this woman had the power to test his control, and it irritated him. Worse...thoughts of her kept him awake nights, and ruined him for any other woman he could easily have bedded. Heaven knew there were a number from whom he could choose.

Except it was Mia's features he wanted to see, the warmth of her smile…and he gently extricated willing fingers, made a seemingly reasonable but regretful excuse and went home alone.

'When we've talked,' Nikolos declared. 'I'll take you home.'

'We have nothing to discuss.'

He brought the vehicle to a halt at a set of traffic lights and turned towards her briefly. 'Yes,' he reiterated hardily. 'We do.'

'Do you insist on a post-mortem with every woman with whom you've had sex?'

The lights changed, and he moved the vehicle forward with the flow of traffic. Minutes later he entered Double Bay and after finding no convenient parking space he swung the car into the entrance of the Ritz-Carlton hotel, requested valet parking, then led her into the hotel lounge.

Refined elegance, she perceived as a waiter hurried forward to usher them to a table, took an order for tea, then unobtrusively retreated.

Mia schooled her features as she deliberately met Nikolos' dark gaze. 'Can we get this over with?'

Was that her voice? She sounded so calm, when inside her nerves were shredding into a tangled mess.

'Why did you leave?'

Her eyes widened slightly, then became shadowed. Twelve weeks had passed since that fateful night, yet every detail was etched in her mind. The magic of his touch, the unleashing of emotions she hadn't known she possessed...

Dear God, how could she have stayed and faced him in the morning? Calmly risen from the bed, showered, dressed, shared breakfast, then walked away as if the night had meant nothing more than the sharing of good sex?

Instead of an earth-shattering experience that had changed her perspective, her life?

'There was no reason to stay.'

'No name, no contact number,' Nikolos pursued silkily. 'No means by which I could get in touch with you. Why?'

'I was unaware there was any protocol involved. What would you have had me write on a note? ''You were great?''' She was on a roll. '''Call me some time and we'll do it again?'' Would that have fed your ego? Salved your conscience?'

He didn't move, but she had the sensation his body coiled like a tightly wound spring.

'You gifted me your virginity. That had to mean something.'

His words were silky smooth and dangerous, and Mia barely repressed a shiver as sensation unfurled deep within at the memory…his disbelief, the husky curse, and his gentleness as he'd led her through the threshold of pain to pleasure beyond her wildest imagination.

And afterwards…dear heaven, *afterwards* he'd held her all night long as she'd become a willing wanton eager for his touch. Again and again.

'It wasn't such a big deal.' And knew she lied...big time.

'No?' His gaze didn't shift.

'The prophylactic broke, remember?'

One of them.

The waiter arrived and laid out their tea, then took his leave.

'If you weren't taking precautions prior to intimacy,' Nikolos continued, 'I imagine you covered any possibility of pregnancy with a prescription for the morning-after pill?'

'I considered it unnecessary.' Foolishly, she accorded in silent self-castigation. What on earth had she been thinking of? Yet when she *had* thought, she'd rationalised her cycle hadn't been in the fertile zone.

So much for the *norm*, the majority!

She became aware of Nikolos' intent gaze, and held it with difficulty.

'And was it unnecessary?' he pursued quietly.

Oh, dear Lord, how did she answer that?

His eyes darkened and assumed a ruthless intensity as her silence stretched too long. 'Mia?'

'My body, my responsibility,' she managed quietly, aware she was just barely holding it together.

'Dammit, you weren't alone in that bed.'

'What do you want me to say? ''Was it as good for you as it was for me?'' Or are you afraid I'll slap you with a paternity suit, demand a large financial settlement, or run to the media and besmirch the Karedes name?' She was like a runaway train that couldn't stop. 'Or maybe all three?'

'The truth will do for a start.'

She held his gaze fearlessly. The *truth*? 'I took a pregnancy test three weeks ago, and had the positive result confirmed by a doctor the following day.'

He waited a beat as he attempted some measure of control. 'Tell me, was I never to know?'

Her hand shook a little as she took time out to add milk to her cup. 'Reality check, Nikolos. Just as you didn't know my name, you hadn't given me yours.'

The breath hissed from his mouth. 'Have you had—?'

'An abortion? No.' The foetus inside her was a living entity. The thought of having it forcibly removed from her body made her feel ill. 'This child is my responsibility.'

'Mine, also. I'll ensure you have specialist obstetrical care, and take care of all medical expenses.'

'I don't want anything from you.'

'If you think I'll walk away from this, you're mistaken.'

'You have no rights—'

'Yes, I do.'

The thought of sharing the child hadn't entered her head. Now that it did, it began to assume gigantic proportion.

'I intend bringing up the child alone.'

'No.'

'What do you mean...*no*? The decision isn't yours to make.'

'The child will bear the Karedes name.'

Mia replaced the cup carefully down onto its saucer, then sank back in her chair. 'Fredrickson,' she corrected.

'*Karedes,*' Nikolos declared with chilling softness.

'As I don't intend changing my surname, *Fredrickson* will appear on the birth certificate.' She rose to her feet and caught up her bag. 'It's been some evening. Your grandmother suspects I've snatched Cris for a toy boy and showed no mercy in her interrogation.' She glared at him, and barely restrained herself from picking up the ashtray and throwing it at him. 'As if that's not enough, you shanghai me and take up where they left off.'

'Sit down.'

'Go to hell.'

'Sit down—please.'

The *please* almost did it, except she refused to give in. 'I'll have the concierge summon a cab.' She fixed him with an angry glare. 'If you try to stop me, I'll—'

'Do what?' Nikolos drawled.

'Call Security and file a harassment charge.'

'You might care to rethink that.'

'Why?' It was a cry from the heart. 'You're bent on detaining me against my will.'

'This conversation would have been better served in private.'

'We've said all there is to say.'

'No,' Nikolos drawled imperturbably. 'We haven't.'

She was tired, she had a headache, and she'd had *enough*. 'It's simple. I'm going to keep the baby. I don't want your help... financial or otherwise. And I'd rather not see you again.'

His appraisal remained steady, and unnerved her...as he meant it to. 'Tough.

Because not seeing me again isn't an option. Nor is refusing my help.'

Mia didn't like his imperturbability, or the hint of elemental ruthlessness beneath his deceptively mild exterior.

Nikolos Karedes possessed an animalistic sense of power that was vaguely frightening. He had no hold over her, no means to force her into any situation she didn't want or covet.

So why did she have the feeling he was intent on taking control? With or without her consent.

It was crazy.

Without a further word she turned and walked to the concierge's desk, requested the attendant summon a cab, then when it swept into the entrance she made her escape.

As the cab eased forward she saw Nikolos emerge from the entrance and lift his hand in silent acknowledgement as he slid behind the wheel of his car.

Any satisfaction she experienced at initiating independence diminished with the knowledge Nikolos Karedes knew who she was, where Alice lived, and her anonymity no longer existed.

CHAPTER THREE

'THE guy you slept with and Cris' *brother* are one and the same? You're kidding me…aren't you?' Alice challenged with a stunned expression as they shared lunch together at a café overlooking the harbour.

It was by way of being a celebration, given Mia had successfully confirmed a three-week placement in a local pharmacy. There was also an indication she'd be offered part-time work during the long summer holidays.

Alice expelled a long drawn-out breath, concern clouding her features. 'Unbelievable.'

A slight understatement, if ever there was one, Mia acknowledged silently. 'It made for an uncomfortable evening.'

'Added to the subtle grilling re your friendship with Cris?'

'*Subtle* didn't enter the equation.' Mia rolled her eyes expressively. 'Cris' grandmother breathed fire and brimstone.'

'A dragon, huh?'

'Oh, yeah. And then some.'

'And?'

She met her sister's gaze, interpreted the silent query, and fielded it. 'You're not going to let up, are you?'

'Got it in one.'

'Nikolos insisted on driving me home, we stopped off for coffee, and we…talked.'

'As in?'

'He asked, I told him, he offered help, I refused,' Mia declared. She paused to sip chilled water from her glass. 'Then I walked out and caught a cab.'

'Not the best move.'

'It seemed a good idea at the time.'

'So what happens now?'

'Nothing, hopefully.'

'You think he's going to dismiss the fact you're carrying a Karedes *heir*?' Alice's voice held a slightly incredulous note.

She'd known for three weeks, and in that time she'd considered the baby *hers*. Her responsibility, therefore her decisions were the only ones that would count.

Now she was forced to accept the father of her child intended to take an active role in its life. Which meant Nikolos Karedes would intrude in *her* life. Something she needed like a hole in the head.

There was a part of her that wanted to cut and run. *Sure,* a tiny imp silently derided. That's *really* going to work!

'You do realise just *who* Nikolos Karedes is, and the power he has in this city?' Alice queried.

A chill shiver slithered the length of Mia's spine. Why did she get the feeling she was losing a battle that had yet to be fought? It was crazy.

If only she hadn't decided to spend the long summer break in Sydney...except she had, and it wasn't possible to go back and change a set of circumstances that had brought her into contact with the man with whom she'd conceived a child.

So...she'd deal with it. All she had to do was remain resolute. Nikolos Karedes might imagine he possessed a few rights. But they had to be limited, surely?

'I'm self-supporting, and entitled to make my own decisions,' Mia reminded gently.

A half-share in their parents' estate had allowed her to purchase her own apartment and have an investment portfolio. An apartment she'd leased out when she'd entered university. Her furniture had been placed in storage, and most of her clothes were stored at Alice's home.

'With regard to yourself,' Alice agreed, frowning with concern. 'However, when it comes to the child, Nikolos Karedes can insist on a DNA test, and with proven paternity he has legal rights with regard to custody, education.'

Mia felt the blood drain from her face. 'You're positive about this?' A ridiculous query, given Alice worked as a para-legal, and possessed an extensive knowledge of the law. 'What if he doesn't choose—'

'To stake a claim?' Her sister paused for a few seconds, then offered gently, 'Hasn't he already stated he intends to be part of the child's life?'

That put a different perspective on going solo. 'So what do you suggest?'

'Establish a convivial friendship with the man.'

'Are you mad?'

Alice shook her head. 'It wouldn't be wise to make an enemy of him.'

The mere thought of him in that role sent a chill shiver feathering the length of her spine, and she placed a protective hand to her waist.

A silent groan of despair rose and died in her throat. How could she have been so foolish as to think she was in control, and able to call the shots?

As to Nikolos Karedes backing down... forget it.

Friends. How could they be friends?

She didn't want to think about it. In fact, she refused to consider anything about the man for the rest of the afternoon.

Mia checked her watch. 'We should go do some shopping before we collect Matt from school.'

'A bid to divert the subject of conversation?'

'Got it in one.'

Alice lifted both hands in a gesture of defeat. 'Okay, time to butt out.'

'No,' Mia contradicted gently. 'I love you dearly, and value your opinion, your advice.'

'But...?'

'I'd prefer not to spend time second-guessing Nikolos Karedes' next move.'

'So let's go enjoy the rest of the day, huh?'

Mia's cellphone pealed within minutes of leaving the café, and she took the call.

'Mia? It's Cris.' His voice held amusement. 'Last night. You and Nikolos. What *was* that?'

If only you knew! 'You could have rescued me.'

'Darling, you were doing just fine on your own.'

'You think?'

'Sweetie, if I was hetero I could almost be jealous of how fast he moved in for the kill. So he drove you home, *and*…?'

'There was no *and*…'

'Of course not. But—'

'I left and took a cab.'

His soft chuckle almost undid her. 'No woman walks out on Nikolos Karedes.'

'This one did.'

'Wish I'd been there.'

'Any fallout from last night?'

'Oh, you could say that.' His humour was infectious. '*Yiayia* lectured me on the age difference, my studies, the family honour. Sofia added her concerns, and brother Nikolos subjected me to one of his discerning looks over breakfast. Incidentally,' he added following a fractional pause. 'Nikolos has your phone number.'

'You gave it to him?' she demanded incredulously.

'You mind?'

Yes, she did. Very much.

'Oh, hell.' Cris swore quietly. 'Want me to go into damage control?'

There was little point. 'No.' She drew in a deep breath, then released it slowly. 'I'm out shopping with Alice.'

'Enjoy. We'll talk soon.'

'Cris?' Alice queried as Mia cut the call.

'Uh-huh.'

'I think,' Alice offered cheerfully, 'we need to do some serious retail therapy.'

'It's that or chocolate,' Mia hinted darkly, and led the way into the next trendy boutique.

It was after four when they arrived home, and it took little prompting for Matt to tend to his homework before dinner.

Mia deposited an assortment of bright carrier bags in her room, then changed into cargo pants and a tee shirt before joining Alice in the kitchen.

They were about to begin preparations for a steak salad when the doorbell rang.

Alice dried her hands, and smoothed a hand over her hair. 'I'll get it.'

A few minutes later she returned carrying a large bouquet of pale roses in cream, peach and apricot. 'For you.'

Mia felt the nerves in her stomach tighten. Who would send her flowers? It couldn't be... She plucked the card, and read the slashing signature.

Nikolos.

No message, just his name.

'Should I guess?' Alice prompted, and Mia shook her head as she extended the card.

'Kind of makes a statement, don't you think?'

'I'll get a vase.'

Mia drew a deep breath and released it slowly. 'How do you feel about discarding dinner and we'll take Matt and go grab a burger? My treat.'

'*Yes.*' Matt's victory gesture clinched it, although his mother added the rider, 'Finish your homework first.'

It was a futile act of defiance, but it felt good as Mia switched off her cellphone *en route* to the nearest burger outlet.

'You think that's going to work?' Alice queried mildly as they collected their order and made for one of the outdoor tables.

'It's something I can control.'

Matt's enthusiasm for a departure in routine was catching, and his natural flair for humour brought laughter during the ride home.

Until Alice turned the car into their street and Mia caught sight of Nikolos' Mercedes parked at the kerb.

'Wow,' Matt breathed with boyish reverence. 'That's right outside our house.'

Mia cursed beneath her breath, and endeavoured to still the nerves turning somersaults inside her stomach. Nikolos emerged from behind the wheel as Alice entered the driveway.

'Let me out before you take the car into the garage,' Mia instructed quietly. 'I'll get rid of him.'

'Don't like your chances.'

It took only seconds to slip out from the car, and she turned to face Nikolos Karedes as the automatic garage door slid closed.

He was too tall, his shoulders too broad…and he was altogether too much. Strong masculine features projected a forceful image that meshed elemental sensuality with leashed strength.

Designer jeans and a chambray shirt replaced the elegant suit and tie of the previous evening, and the casual look in no way diminished his animalistic aura of power.

Mia took in the faint grooves slashing his cheeks, the tiny lines fanning out from his eyes, the curve of his mouth, and conducted a mental count to five as she attempted to slow her heartbeat.

Attack was the best form of defence…wasn't it? 'What are you doing here?'

'You left me little choice,' Nikolos drawled. 'Your sister's answering machine wasn't activated, and your cellphone is switched off.'

'We were out.' With the obvious intention of being incommunicado. She should have known he wouldn't let it rest for long. 'We said all there was to say last night.'

'No,' Nikolos drawled. 'We didn't. You chose to leave before we were done.'

Her fingers curled into a tight fist. 'I have nothing more to say to you.'

He glanced towards the neat fences, the surrounding houses. 'I suggest we have this conversation elsewhere.'

'Why?' Mia demanded, sorely tried.

No one had worked their way beneath her skin as this man did. She was incredibly aware of his sensual alchemy and the effect it had on her. Potent, devastating and infinitely dangerous. She could recall in vivid detail how it felt to have his mouth possess her own, the touch of his hands on her body...how he could make her *feel*.

She didn't want to go there. Didn't want to remember. Not in the daylight hours. It was bad enough he haunted her dreams, invaded her subconscious, and lingered there all through each night.

'We're going to share a child together.'

Her eyes flared, widening into deep dark pools as she regarded him. '*I'm* the one who's pregnant. Whose body will nurture and expel the child into the world, feed and care for it.'

His expression didn't change. 'All the more reason for us to take time to get to know each other better.'

She waited a beat. 'I think we've already taken care of that, don't you?'

One eyebrow slanted. 'One night of intimacy doesn't constitute a relationship.'

'There isn't going to be a *relationship*!'

'Friends,' he amended. 'It would be a start, don't you think?'

'A start to *what*?' She was on a roll. 'Civility? Sharing the occasional meal, observing the social niceties? I don't think so!'

'What are you afraid of?'

Oh, man, you can't begin to comprehend! 'I don't see it would serve any purpose.'

'You didn't answer the question.'

Mia heard a slight sound and turned to see Alice framed in the open doorway, a polite smile creasing her attractive features.

'Hi, I'm Alice. You must be Nikolos.' The smile curved a little wider. 'Perhaps you'd like to take this indoors and continue your conversation over coffee.'

Coffee? Indoors? *Are you mad?* Mia demanded silently, and met Alice's bland expression as Nikolos inclined his head.

'Thank you.'

Matt's boyish enthusiasm acted as a merciful distraction, and within minutes Mia followed Alice into the kitchen.

'Traitor,' she accused quietly as she took down cups and set them on matching saucers.

'You could hardly stand out on the lawn indefinitely.'

'Want to bet?'

It didn't take long for the coffee to percolate, and Matt leapt to his feet the instant Alice appeared in the lounge.

'Nikolos has a cruiser.' His eyes gleamed with excitement. 'Guess what? He said we can all go out on it. With him. Sunday.' He was trying hard to act cool. 'If it's okay.'

'That's nice of him.'

Nice? Mia sent Nikolos a dark glance that intimated she knew exactly what game he was playing. The mere thought of spending a day in his company set the nerves inside her stomach turning somersaults. It wasn't a comfortable feeling!

'We can go, can't we?'

Mia could see Alice wavering towards acceptance. Understandably, given Matt's enthusiasm. He was such a great kid, and he didn't deserve to be denied a wonderful day's outing.

'Mia?'

Sibling loyalty at its best, for it gave her the opportunity to decline. One Nikolos Karedes expected her to take, she perceived, from the faint challenge evident in his dark gaze.

The very reason she summoned a smile. 'How could I be the one to disappoint my favourite nephew?'

Matt's response was a joyful whoop.

A day spent in Nikolos' company. How hard could it be, given her sister and nephew would be there as a buffer?

Nikolos finished his coffee, then rose to his feet and took his leave.

'I'll collect you on the way to the marina on Sunday morning. Shall we say nine?'

Mission accomplished, Mia accorded silently as Alice accompanied him to the front entrance. With determined effort she stacked cups and saucers together and took them through to the kitchen.

Alice joined her there minutes later, and they regarded each other in silence for a few seconds.

'Don't hold back,' Mia offered quietly, and Alice rolled her eyes.

'For what it's worth, I don't think you have a snowflake's chance in hell of dismissing him from your life.'

'You base that opinion after having spent ten minutes in his company?'

'Intuition?' Alice ventured, and took time to check her watch. 'I'll organise Matt off to bed. Give me ten minutes.'

'More coffee? Or tea?'

'Tea.'

Mia took care of the dishes, and was in the process of pouring tea into two large mugs when Alice entered the kitchen.

'Shall we take this into the lounge? Maybe slot in a DVD and view a movie? Or do you want to talk?'

Mia shot her sister a faintly rueful smile. 'A movie.'

'You're on.'

They sat together in companionable silence as the movie played, and when it was over they closed everything down and went to their separate rooms.

CHAPTER FOUR

SUNDAY held the promise of being a beautiful day, the sun ascending in a cloudless blue sky. A gentle breeze moved the air, dappling the water's surface as Nikolos eased the powerful cruiser out into the harbour.

Wow had been Matt's appreciative description when Nikolos had led them to the large boat at its marina mooring.

Fitting, Mia agreed, for a seaworthy vehicle of sufficient size to hold several passengers and throw a small party.

Splendid accoutrements with fine attention to detail, it was an expensive craft only the wealthy could afford.

'You could live here,' Matt declared, attaching himself to Nikolos' side. 'And go anywhere.'

'I don't get to use it very often. Mostly it gets chartered out for private entertaining.'

Doubtless at an exorbitant fee.

'Matt appears to have nominated Nikolos as his new idol.'

Mia encountered Alice's regretful glance. 'He doesn't get to be around men very often.'

'Today he has two,' she offered lightly, watching as Cris took over the wheel and left Nikolos free to point out places of interest.

She had to admit he appeared to have a natural empathy with her nephew, providing information with casual grace for a young brain eager to soak up knowledge about the cruiser, its measurements, capacity, engine.

Yet, despite its size, Mia was very aware of being trapped in a relatively small space out on the water with no escape until Nikolos brought the cruiser in to berth late that after-noon…seven, eight hours from now.

Alice, Matt and Cris provided a welcome distraction, although she had to wonder if her emotional tension was evident. She hoped not!

Nikolos was *there*, the focus of her existence, and she was incredibly aware of his every move, each glance, the depth of his dark gaze whenever it came to rest on her.

Thank heaven for sunglasses, for they served a dual purpose in shading her expressive eyes. Although it worked both ways... she couldn't determine his expression, either!

Yet being in such close proximity brought alive the sexual chemistry they shared, until it almost became a palpable entity.

Every nerve-cell in her body tautened to screaming point, and she was conscious of every breath she took.

It was maddening to be so aware of him, to retain such a vivid memory of what it felt like to be held in his arms...his scent, the feel and taste of his skin beneath her lips. And to know she wanted his touch. Craved it, in a manner she found vaguely shocking.

Did he guess? Dear heaven, she hoped not!

Sydney was her home town, the city where she'd grown up, and she thought she knew its origins, the history behind the harbour bridge, the dramas associated with the design and building of the famed Opera House.

Yet she became fascinated as Nikolos had Cris take the wheel while he gave Matt a verbal recount, and pointed out places of interest.

'Mia, come look at this!'

Matt's excited voice brooked little resistance as Mia followed Alice to where Matt stood.

'See that house? Nikolos said a former prime minister lived there.'

She was barely conscious of a subtle shift in position, only that Nikolos had somehow moved to stand beside her, his solid frame close to her own.

Too close, Mia decided as his arm brushed hers when he pointed out the home belonging to a famous Australian actress.

Was his touch deliberate, or was she merely being fanciful?

Seconds later there was little doubt as he slid an arm around her waist, lingered there, then smoothed a path up her back to capture her shoulder.

It was fleeting, outwardly casual to any onlooker. Except she felt all her skin-cells leap into tingling life, and she suppressed a shivery sensation threatening to wreak visible havoc.

What was *wrong* with her? It wasn't possible for one person to have such a devastating effect on another…was it?

Mia wanted to move away. Yet conversely, she needed to stay. If nothing else, to prove she could.

Nikolos Karedes knew precisely what he was doing, and she refused to give him an atom of satisfaction.

Yet, despite her calm exterior, inside she was a mass of nerves. Breathing was an automatic act, yet she became conscious of every breath she took, each exhalation.

Once, she could have sworn his breath teased her hair when he moved to stand behind her, and her whole body stiffened as he leant forward and grasped the rail, effectively caging her in.

The temptation to dig an elbow into his ribs was impossible to resist, and she'd barely congratulated herself on the small victory when she felt the imprint of his body against her own.

It lasted only seconds, but it was enough to lock the breath in her throat.

She could *kill* him…and would, she determined, at the first opportunity.

Almost as if he *knew*, he moved away and placed a hand on Matt's shoulder. 'How about we relieve Cris at the wheel?'

Matt's response was immediate. 'We? As in you and me?'

'Sure. Are you up for it?'

As if Matt needed to be asked! His face was a study in pride, pleasure and euphoria as Nikolos allowed him to feel the powerful engine beneath his hands as he stood in front of Nikolos at the wheel.

'He sure knows how to capture a young boy's heart,' Mia voiced lightly as Cris joined her, and incurred his musing look.

'Afraid he might use similar tactics to capture yours?'

'My interest doesn't rest with cruiser specifications.'

Cris' expression sobered. 'Nikolos has a reputation as a skilled negotiator, and he can be ruthlessly tenacious when it comes to getting what he wants.'

'You're telling me this, because…?'

'He wants you,' he stated simply.

The engine stilled, and Cris checked his watch. 'We've stopped for lunch.'

Alice had insisted on preparing a picnic hamper filled with a variety of salads, bread, and home-baked fruit pies. Nikolos withdrew cooked chicken and cold cuts from the cabin fridge, and retrieved chilled drinks.

A retractable table and collapsible wooden chairs on the main deck made for a relaxed atmosphere, and it was much more informal than eating in the main cabin lounge/dining area.

Matt was in his element, his natural curiosity endearing as he plied Nikolos and Cris with numerous questions. Cars, boats, countries they'd visited.

'And you, Mia?' Nikolos queried with apparent idleness. 'Any places of interest you particularly enjoyed?'

'New York, Hawaii.' She cast Alice an affectionate glance. 'Paris.'

'It's a beautiful city,' Cris relayed. 'Friendly people, great food, fantastic ambience. Especially in the south.'

'Mia can speak French. She does martial arts, too,' Matt declared in a bid to impart information about his favourite and only aunt. 'Mum and I went to watch her in competition. She's awesome.'

Mia bore Nikolos' interested gaze with equanimity.

'Any other hidden talents?' he drawled. When she refrained from answering he transferred his attention to Alice, who merely grinned as she offered, 'You expect me to risk my life?'

His sensually moulded mouth curved to form a musing smile as he countered, 'Family loyalty?'

'Self-preservation,' Mia answered on her sister's behalf.

In retrospect it was a carefree day spent in convivial company, and for Mia it was wonderful to see Alice relax and enjoy herself, while Matt's pleasure was a matter of pure delight.

It more than made up for spending several hours in Nikolos' presence, for she acutely aware of him in a way that tied her nerves in countless knots.

Did he know? Dear heaven, she hoped not.

She'd never experienced this depth of emotion before, or felt so mentally and emotionally attuned to anyone to quite this degree.

It wasn't a feeling she coveted. It was almost sickening. Then she held back the laugh threatening to burst from her throat. Was there such a thing as lust-sick?

Honesty compelled her to admit she wanted his touch. To be able to experience again the depth of emotion, the heat...Why not call it how it was—the *ecstasy* she experienced in his arms.

How could she be so intensely vulnerable? So weak? It was ridiculous.

Consequently it was something of a relief when Nikolos eased the cruiser into its berth at the marina.

'Do you need to clean out the bilges?' Matt queried as they disembarked, his eagerness to help clearly apparent.

Nikolos ruffled the boy's hair. 'The marina staff take care of it. You can come with me to the office when I hand over the keys if you like, while Cris goes ahead with your mother and Mia to the car.'

'I think *idol* just moved up to *god,*' Mia murmured as they reached the car park.

'He's a great kid,' Cris complimented as he unlocked the boot and stowed their gear. 'We'll take him out again.'

'That's so kind. He's had such a wonderful time. We all have.' Alice's enthusiasm had Mia silencing a protesting groan.

What hope did she have of minimising her contact with Nikolos, when he already had Alice and Matt on side?

Minutes later she turned and saw Nikolos and Matt walking towards them. Her stomach lurched at the sight of man and boy together, and her mind took a quantum leap into the future. To the years ahead when Nikolos would spend time with their son or daughter.

She saw all too clearly how Nikolos would swing their child high onto his shoulders, the laughter, the fun they'd share together. The affection, the love.

Yet a child spending equal time with each parent, emotionally torn between both. Probably with step-parents and step-siblings to cope with, and perhaps resentment at not belonging to one family or the other.

It wasn't an ideal picture, and for a brief moment she felt stricken at the implications of what the future might hold.

Matt's excited voice intruded, and Mia summoned an affectionate smile as he drew close. It would be wonderful to return to the simplicity of being a child, she mused. To have the unconditional love of a parent, few complications in life, to seize the day and squeeze the most enjoyment possible from it.

She caught Nikolos' intent gaze, met and held it for a few timeless seconds, grateful for the dark lenses shading her eyes so their expression remained indiscernible.

It was almost six when Nikolos turned into Alice's driveway. Summer daylight saving meant it would be light for two, perhaps three more hours.

Mia determined to engage Matt in a few games of chess. It would help focus her mind on something other than the tall, powerful man who seemed intent on turning her life upside down.

'Thanks for a wonderful day.' Alice's and Matt's voices echoed in tandem, and Nikolos smiled as Mia added her own.

'I have tickets to a private gallery showing on Tuesday evening. A percentage of the ticket price and sold items will be donated to one of the charities the Karedes family are known to sponsor. I'd like to invite you both as my guests.'

'Alice?' Please say you can't get someone to sit with Matt at such short notice, she begged silently.

'That would be lovely. Matt is due to have a sleep-over with a friend.' Alice's features creased with friendly warmth. 'Can I check and have Mia confirm with you?'

'Of course.'

Mia crossed to the rear of the car to retrieve the picnic basket, aware Nikolos fell into step beside her.

'You're not playing fair,' she accused quietly.

'No?' He undid the boot and they both reached for the basket simultaneously.

Nikolos' fingers brushed her own, and her skin cells felt as if they burned from the contact.

'I'll be in touch,' he drawled as she turned away and began walking up the path.

She didn't look back as the car engine purred to life, and she declined to join Alice and Matt as they waved a friendly farewell.

'Wasn't it a cool day?' Matt queried seconds later. 'That cruiser is something else. Nikolos is a great guy. I like him.'

'Go wash up,' Alice bade. 'While Mia and I organise something to eat.'

'On my way.'

'You look as if you want to bite my head off,' Alice said as soon as Matt was out of earshot.

Oh, hell. She made an attempt at humour. 'Is it that obvious?'

'I'm your sister, remember?'

And far too perceptive for Mia's peace of mind. 'I'd prefer to keep any contact with Nikolos Karedes to a minimum.'

Alice's eyes were startlingly direct. 'Can't you see he's not going to give up?'

'I have no intention of accepting every invitation he extends, just because—' She paused, and Alice completed the sentence.

'You're carrying his child?'

'Yes, dammit!'

'You'd like it better if I renege Tuesday evening, and you show as his partner?'

'You know the answer to that one.'

Alice arched an eyebrow. 'So?'

Matt's appearance in the kitchen saved Mia from elaborating further.

Their evening meal comprised cold cuts and a salad followed by fresh fruit, and afterwards Mia suggested chess.

'Loser gets to take out the trash for the next week.'

Matt rose to the challenge with a grin. 'Guess that's going to be you.'

'Want to bet?'

Alice called a halt at eight-thirty. 'Time for bed, Matt.'

'I'm about to sweep Mia off the board,' he protested, and gained a five-minute reprieve.

'Yay!' He raised a fist in the air in triumph.

Mia spread her hands. 'Tomorrow night I get to win.'

He gave her an infectious grin. 'In your dreams.'

She reached forward and mussed his hair. 'Make sure yours are good ones.'

'You, too.' He picked up the chessmen and packed them away. 'Goodnight.'

Mia cleared away the teacups and stifled a yawn as she stacked the dishwasher, glancing up as Alice re-entered the kitchen.

'If you don't mind, I'll grab a shower, then have an early night.'

'All that fresh sea air,' her sister declared sagely.

'Uh-huh.' Not to mention a day fraught with tension.

Nikolos Karedes had a lot to answer for, Mia determined as she slid into bed. His powerful image filled her conscious mind, and even in sleep he invaded her dreams... haunting evocative sequences that left her wanting.

The privately owned gallery catered to the social élite whose main purpose in life was undoubtedly to be seen at events such as this, Mia perceived as she glanced in idle speculation around the large, elegantly furnished room.

Works of art graced the walls, occupied strategically placed stands, displayed with deliberate precision.

Invitation only, the evening's exhibition featured works by three of the city's well-known artists.

'Alice, how nice to see you here.'

Mia glanced at the immaculately attired man who greeted her sister, and offered a smile as Alice introduced him.

'Craig Mitchell. A legal partner and my boss.'

Mia noted the faintly heightened colour tingeing Alice's cheeks, and lifted an eyebrow in silent speculation when he moved away.

'Don't even go there,' Alice warned quietly, and Mia's mouth curved a little.

'Hidden interest?'

'No.'

And cows jumped over the moon, she accorded silently as she cast her sister a speculative glance. 'Uh-huh.'

'It's quite a gathering, isn't it?'

Mia had to agree. 'A collection of the beautiful people dressed in their finest.' She sipped chilled water from her glass, and could almost have wished for something stronger.

'Speaking of which,' Alice voiced quietly, 'one of the most stunning women in this room is moving this way.'

Stunning didn't quite cover it, she decided as she followed her sister's line of vision. A model? Actress? Certainly no ordinary mortal. Tall, long flowing dark hair, classically moulded features, and beautifully attired in a black figure-hugging gown.

Exquisite make-up, Mia added as she drew close, aware just how long it took to create such perfection.

'Nikolos.'

Oh, my. Sultry tones with the hint of an accent she couldn't begin to place. And a proprietorial manner that irked as much as it irritated.

Mia watched as Nikolos turned towards the sable-haired beauty, and saw his features crease into a polite smile.

'Anouska.'

He was good. Skilled, she amended, in the art of social behaviour. So adept, she had little idea whether the exquisite female was friend, acquaintance, or lover. The next question had to be past or present?

Anouska inclined her head towards Cris.

'Home for the holidays?'

'Yes.'

Anouska returned her attention to Nikolos. 'Friends from out of town, darling?' The faintly languid drawl held a teasing quality as she arched an enquiring eyebrow.

'Mia,' Nikolos indicated by way of introduction. 'And her sister Alice.'

Anouska's smile was a mere shadow as she subjected Mia to an encompassing appraisal. 'Should I know you?'

Cris offered, 'Mia is—'

'The mother of my unborn child,' Nikolos concluded quietly.

Mia felt as if everything faded from the periphery of her vision. There was only their small tableau, five people momentarily frozen in time.

The illusion lasted mere seconds, and was broken as Nikolos caught Mia's hand in his and lifted it to his lips.

What was he doing?

She promised herself she'd do him physical harm at the first opportunity.

The room and its occupants came back into focus, together with the background chatter. She glimpsed Cris mime a silent whistle, and Alice appeared to be holding her breath.

'Really, darling,' Anouska protested lightly. 'Your sense of humour is questionable.'

Nikolos' expression didn't change. 'Humour wasn't my intention.'

Mia attempted to tug her hand free, only to have Nikolos tighten his hold.

A malevolent gleam appeared so fleetingly in Anouska's dark eyes, Mia had to wonder if she imagined it.

'You've kept her well hidden, darling. There hasn't been so much as a whisper of any one of several women who might have any—'Anouska paused with a delicate lift of one eyebrow '—shall we say *meaning* in your life.'

Ouch! Sour grapes were never attractive.

'Understandable,' Nikolos drawled. 'Given I prefer to keep my private life—' his pause was deliberate '—private.'

Anouska didn't bat an eyelid. 'Can we assume there will be a shotgun wedding in the near future?'

Forget sour grapes, Mia dismissed silently. The woman might take the cake in the stunning stakes, but her tongue was pure acid.

'No doubt word will circulate when I've been able to persuade Mia to make an honest man of me.'

He was ice, to an almost frightening degree. Lethal, whom only a fool would choose to have as an adversary.

'Something I'm disinclined to do,' Mia offered in an attempt to set the record straight.

'How…amazingly unperceptive of you.'

'Yes,' Mia said sweetly. 'But then, my values verge towards the unusual.' She visualised a mental high-five. Score one for Mia! It was easy to summon a winsome smile. 'If you'll excuse me? I should go examine the exhibits.'

Nikolos made no move to relinquish her hand as he chose to walk at her side, and she waited only seconds before bursting into restrained speech.

'Just what did you think you were doing back there?'

Amusement tugged the edges of his mouth. 'Shall we say…setting the record straight?'

'Really?' Cool, she could do *cool*. 'And that's necessary…because?'

'I have no reason to hide the fact we've made a child together.'

'I'll have returned to Brisbane before my pregnancy is visible.'

His gaze was startlingly direct. 'No, you won't.'

'Excuse me?' It was amazing she managed to keep her voice calm.

'You heard.'

Her eyes glittered with indignation. 'I have a commitment—'

'To complete your registration examinations at the end of next year,' Nikolos completed. 'Something which can be arranged here. As can your assigned pharmacy placements.'

'You've made enquiries?'

One eyebrow lifted, and his mouth assumed a mocking curve. 'Did you think I wouldn't?'

She shot him a glare that would have felled a lesser man. 'You have no right—'

'Yes, I do,' he said quietly.

Alice's cautious reminder of legal fact backed up by DNA returned to haunt her. 'After the birth,' she qualified tightly, wondering how on earth she would cope with seeing Nikolos on a regular basis, much less relinquishing her child to him for regular custody visits.

His fingers threaded through her own, and tightened when she attempted to pull free.

'Must you?'

'Is it such a hardship to present a united front?'

Mia contrived for superficial serenity, and achieved it...just. 'I don't like playing games.'

'Who said it was a game?'

She swallowed the lump that rose in her throat, aware the conversation had taken a subtle shift, and she became intensely conscious of his close proximity.

The scent of him, a combination of male muskiness and expensive cologne mixing with the clean smell of freshly laundered clothes.

It was all too easy to visualise the hard body beneath the trappings of his fine tailored apparel. Broad-shouldered, lean-hipped, the chiselled perfection of well-honed muscles, how they flexed with each move he made, the washboard stomach and tight butt.

'Would you deny me the pleasure of seeing our child grow inside you?'

Oh, dear heaven. Heat suffused her veins at the mere thought of its conception. How she lay awake night after night reliving in vivid detail the touch of Nikolos' hands, his mouth, each caress...the electrifying passion they'd shared several times through the dark hours, until the first light of dawn when she'd quietly dressed and slipped silently from his room.

It was too much. *He* was too much.

'By making a public statement, you've irretrievably connected the two of us together. Something you could easily have avoided.' She met his gaze and held it. 'So why didn't you?'

He slanted her a musing glance. 'To ensure there's no doubt to whom you belong.' He paused fractionally, then added quietly, 'Or to whom I owe my loyalty.'

She got it in one. 'Anouska.'

His eyes speared hers, dark and unfathomable. 'You doubt I can handle Anouska?'

'No.' He could handle anyone he chose, undoubtedly with chilling efficiency. She just didn't want to be one of them.

Where had that come from?

She wasn't *falling* for him…was she? A hollow laugh rose and died in her throat. Who was she fooling?

Could he guess at the state of her emotions? The utter turmoil he'd caused? Or were her hormones adding to the mix?

'What do you think?'

Mia registered Nikolos' voice and dragged her attention back to the exotic landscape displayed in splendid isolation.

Bold colours apparently splashed at random on canvas, but somehow meshing to depict a scene that captured and held the imagination.

'It would need a room all of its own,' she ventured, and listened as he discussed the artist with knowledgeable expertise of his work.

They moved from one exhibit to another, pausing every now and then to devote more than a passing examination of anything that took their interest.

'I have tickets for the Thursday evening performance of *The Merry Widow*,' Nikolos intimated as they reached the last exhibit.

Mia turned towards him. 'Are you asking me out?'

'Yes.'

'On a date?'

'Is that so strange?'

Just the two of them, alone, with neither Cris nor Alice as a buffer.

'You need to think about it?'

She met his teasing gaze, and summoned a brilliant smile. 'No.'

'Is that a no you don't need to think about it, or no you refuse?'

'I'd enjoy a night at the theatre.'

A flashlight exploded close by, one of a series of flashes as a photographer captured shots for the social pages.

Nikolos Karedes was newsworthy, so it was a given his photo would feature among those of the city's social echelon.

Doubtless the appearance of an unknown woman at his side would cause conjecture. Mia wondered just how long it would take for the rumour mill to begin its speculative journey, and how much fact would be among the fiction.

Worse, what would Sofia's reaction be when she checked the social pages, and news of Nikolos' revelation reached her ears? As it would.

'Sofia, Angelena and Cris are aware of the situation.'

Oh, heavens, he'd *told* them? 'You read minds?'

'You possess expressive features.'

Oh, *great*. Just what she wanted to hear. 'Thanks.'

He'd set the cat among the pigeons. She could almost hear the flutter and flapping of wings as the Karedes matriarchs absorbed the news.

'Naturally they expect to resume their acquaintance with you.'

'I don't think I'm ready for another interrogation just yet.'

His husky laughter came as a surprise. 'I promise not to leave you alone with them.'

'That's what worries me.'

'My mother will adore you. You're providing her with a longed-for grandchild. And Angelena is a pussycat at heart.'

'You could have fooled me.'

She watched idly as Anouska posed with professional ease and exchanged a few words with the photographer.

Ensuring the man noted the designer label she wore? Or that her feet were shod in Manolo Blahnik's?

Doubtless such detail bore importance, Mia accorded with unaccustomed cynicism.

It took a while to circulate the room, for many of the guests were associates and business acquaintances who used such social occasions to touch base.

Mia smiled and indulged in polite conversation with each introduction, fielding the subtle and not so subtle queries thinly disguised as an exchange of social pleasantries.

It was a relief when the evening drew to a close following an announcement that record funds had been raised to benefit the nominated charity.

The guests began to disperse, and Mia slid into the passenger seat, silent as Nikolos sent the car whispering through the city streets.

Alice, ever the polite hostess, offered coffee when the car drew to a halt in her driveway, and Mia held her breath hoping, praying Nikolos would decline.

'It's kind of you, but I have to catch an early morning flight to Melbourne. Another time?'

Minutes later she followed Alice indoors, pausing in the lounge to step out of her stilettos.

Alice copied her actions, then offered a level glance. 'Want to talk?'

She felt all talked out, and tiredness seemed to close around her like a shroud. 'Can I take a rain check?'

'Of course.' Alice's features held concern. 'You look beat. Try to get a good night's sleep.'

As if that were likely to happen. She'd probably lie awake replaying the evening over and over in her mind.

CHAPTER FIVE

MUCH to Mia's surprise she slept well, and woke feeling relatively refreshed. She could smell fresh coffee, and longed for it, except caffeine was a no-no.

Today she and Alice were just going to potter around the house completing chores, talk, and simply relax.

It made for a leisurely day, and one they enjoyed. Alice's week off from work would soon end, and, with Mia's holiday employment about to begin, it was pleasant to fill the cookie tins, freeze muffins for Matt's school lunches, and simply catch up.

Nikolos Karedes didn't get a mention, and that suited Mia just fine.

There were a few friends she needed to touch base with, and she made the requisite phone calls, checked with the leasing agent who handled her apartment, and took in a movie with Alice next day.

It felt strange to be embarking on a date with Nikolos. There was a part of her that wanted to opt out. The unwise part urged her to throw caution to the wind and go with it.

How difficult could it be? They'd attend a lauded theatre production, he'd drive her home, she'd offer polite thanks…and the evening would be done.

Who do you think you're kidding? Mia queried silently as she selected deep red silk evening trousers with matching camisole and jacket, slipped her feet into stiletto-heeled sandals, and added minimum jewellery.

Already her nerves were every which way but loose, and she was conscious of every breath she took as she slid into the passenger seat of his luxurious car.

Emotional havoc reigned as raw passion swirled deep within, spinning its sensual web. It was madness, utter insanity to be so affected by him and the intense sexual chemistry he was able to generate.

Fate and circumstance had thrown them together once, and now they were bent on showing their hand again. This time she wouldn't be able to cut and run, for her connection with Nikolos was forged by virtue of the child she carried.

'When did you return from Melbourne?' It seemed a logical query, and she met his musing glance as he paused at an intersection.

'The late-afternoon flight.'

'I imagine it was a successful trip?'

'Yes.' Intense negotiations, a particularly stubborn adversary who knew he had nowhere to go, but determined to play hardball just for the hell of it.

'I imagine you travel frequently?'

'It's an integral part of my position as head of the Karedes empire.'

Did he have a woman waiting for him in a number of cities around the world?

'No.'

His quiet drawl startled her. 'I beg your pardon?'

'I don't bed women indiscriminately.'

'You expect me to believe I was an exception?'

'It was an exceptional night.' He waited a beat. 'For both of us.'

And then some. She retained every second of it... The faint prickling sensation at the base of her neck; how she'd glanced away from the group she'd been with and met his gaze, literally across the crowded room, and felt as if she'd been struck by an electrical force so strong she'd become powerless to move.

He'd threaded his way through the mingling guests and engaged her in conversation...and never left her side for what remained of the evening.

Afterwards she'd accepted his invitation to share coffee in the lounge of his hotel. Even then she'd known how she wanted the evening to end. The excitement, apprehension…and the passion. To explore the previously unexplored with this man.

It had been…unbelievable. He was unbelievable. She'd forgotten who or where she was, or why. There had been only *him*, the night, and the most wonderful experience of her life.

Mia focused her attention beyond the windscreen, and chose silence until they reached the theatre foyer, where patrons merged and mingled while waiters circulated offering champagne and orange juice.

She recognised a few of the well-known glitterati, aware of Nikolos Karedes' position among the élite social set.

To be seen at his side, socially, undoubtedly caused speculative interest among his contemporaries. Introductions and polite conversation became the order of the hour, and she began to wish she could sip something stronger than orange juice as Anouska swanned into view looking as if she'd stepped straight from the cover of *Vogue* magazine.

Her gown was one of those barely there creations in tangerine silk…strapless, backless, and moulded her slender curves to perfection.

'There you are, darling.' The husky tones were exactly as Mia remembered. So too was the smile, the seemingly liquid dark eyes expressing blatant sensuality…and the body language that of a woman on the make.

Oh, my, this was going to be some evening!

'Anouska.' Mia was so polite, it was almost a travesty.

'Mya…or is it Mary?'

This could only get worse. 'Mia.' The correction held a faint emphasis that caused the woman's eyes to narrow slightly before she redirected her attention.

'Nikolos. Such a shame I couldn't join you in Melbourne. The boutique. Scheduled invitation-only fashion showing. You know how it is?' She lifted an elegant shoulder. 'Maybe next time?'

So it was war, huh? One-sided, but war nonetheless.

'I don't recall issuing an invitation.' Nikolos' voice held a degree of wry cynicism Anouska chose to ignore.

'Darling—' the protest was prettily voiced and accompanied by an alluring smile '—since when did I need one?'

Saved by the bell…or, more pertinent, the electronic buzzer, Mia breathed with relief.

Short-lived, she determined as Anouska accompanied them into the auditorium and took the same row.

Nikolos indicated their seats, and Mia deliberately took the one farthest of the two, aware the fashionista slid into the seat immediately adjacent his.

Oh, this was going to be just peachy! The mistress on one side, with the mother of his unborn child on the other.

'Maybe I should leave?' she queried in an undertone as the orchestra set up.

Nikolos leaned in close. 'Don't even think about it.'

He was close, too close. If she turned her head, his lips would almost brush hers.

'She has prior claim.'

'No, she doesn't.'

'Like I care?'

He caught hold of her hand, and held it fast within his own. When she endeavoured to break free, he traced the delicate veins at her wrist in a gesture meant to soothe.

Mia's response was to dig her nails in *hard*. Not that it had the slightest effect, for Nikolos merely enclosed her hand within both of his.

The curtain rose, and it became all too easy to lose herself in the magical production, the actors, the singing.

Scene changes were slick, and intermission came far too quickly, breaking the spell.

Anouska rose to her feet. 'Coming out for a drink, darling?'

'Not for me,' Mia negated politely, and offered Nikolos a stunning smile. 'But don't let that stop you.'

'Nikolos?' The tone held an edge of impatience Nikolos chose to ignore.

'Don't wait for us.'

Anouska gave an imperceptible shrug and eased her way into the aisle.

'Playing games comes with a price.'

'Really?' Mia didn't miss a beat. 'Anouska has a neon sign with *mine* pasted to her forehead whenever she's near you. Or hadn't you noticed?'

'She owns an exclusive fashion boutique in Double Bay,' he informed silkily. 'We're social acquaintances, nothing more.'

'Really?'

His eyes narrowed. 'You disbelieve me?'

'I didn't say that.'

'If I owed loyalty to another woman, I would not have—'

'Seduced me?' Mia intercepted. 'Let's tell it like it was.'

'My memory recall has it as being entirely mutual.'

That night would haunt her for the rest of her life. She swallowed the slight lump that had risen in her throat. 'Okay, so it was mutual.'

A faint smile curved the edges of his mouth. 'Such honesty.'

Mia rose to her feet. 'I think I need some fresh air. On my own,' she added as he joined her.

'Forget it.'

'I don't need anyone to hold my hand.'

'Tough.'

Her eyes flared with withheld anger. 'You really are the—'

His mouth closed over hers in a kiss that tore the words from her throat as his tongue swept briefly over hers, tasted, lingered, then withdrew, leaving her speechless.

'You've walked out on me twice,' Nikolos said quietly. 'I don't aim to let you do it again.'

Mia didn't offer so much as a word, for there wasn't one coherent thought in her head at that precise moment.

She was too aware of the taste and feel of him. And worse, much worse, was the urge to pull his head down to hers and repossess his mouth.

There were people in the auditorium...witness to the electric tension fizzing between Nikolos Karedes and his unknown companion.

She told herself she didn't care, but she did, and hated the soft colour suffusing her cheeks as she preceded him into the crowded foyer.

Locating the powder room was easy, and waiting in line provided sufficient time for her to regain a sense of relative calm.

Nikolos was there when she re-emerged into the foyer, and she walked silently at his side as they returned to their seats.

Anouska sent her a killing glance as the curtain lifted, and, although Mia did her best to dismiss the woman's expressed venom, it stayed with her through much of the final half of the production.

There were occasions when she'd been the victim of envy, even jealousy. But nothing she'd experienced came close to the momentary hatred visible in Anouska's eyes.

The message was plain...*Watch your back.*

It was a relief when the curtain came down after a resounding ovation, and they made a move to leave.

Anouska placed a hand on Nikolos' arm. 'Coffee at the usual place?'

Are you kidding?

Nikolos removed her hand. 'I think not.'

The fashionista offered a conciliatory moue. 'Can't be much fun, darling, having a pregnant mistress.' She leant towards Mia with apparent concern. 'Morning sickness, tiredness...how are you coping?'

'Well, thank you,' Mia responded sweetly. She cast Nikolos a winsome smile. 'I can easily get a cab home if you want to share coffee with your friends.'

'No.'

Anouska's eyes widened with playful coquetry. 'If Mia's happy…' she let her voice trail deliberately '…to allow you an open relationship?' She lifted her shoulders and formed a seductive smile. 'Darling, you know where I am.'

Talk about eating a man alive!

'What do you think you're doing?' Nikolos demanded with deceptive mildness the instant Anouska was out of earshot.

Mia spared him a telling look that had no effect whatsoever. 'Returning the favour.'

'For?'

'Setting the cat among the pigeons.'

They cleared the foyer and reached the street. Nikolos' car was in secure parking, and they walked at a leisurely pace.

'Would you like to go somewhere for a drink?' Nikolos queried as he eased the powerful vehicle into the flow of traffic.

'Why not?' she managed lightly. It had begun as a date...they might as well finish the evening as one.

'You aren't going to add the proviso as long as it's not one of Anouska's favoured haunts?'

'I was hoping you'd figure that out for yourself.'

His husky laughter caused sensation to feather its way down her spine.

Nikolos chose a trendy café on the city outskirts, and placed an order for tea and coffee as soon as they were seated.

'So,' he began idly, holding her gaze. 'Why don't you tell me something about yourself?'

'Such as?'

His mouth curved to form a musing smile. 'Why not start at the beginning?'

'You mean you haven't had me investigated?' she queried with unaccustomed cynicism.

He wasn't about to tell her that no one managed to gain access to the Karedes inner family circle without security measures being observed.

The waiter delivered their order, his service faultless as he set down condiments.

Nikolos reached forward and poured her tea, added milk and sugar. It was a surprisingly unexpected gesture.

'I know you chose to study pharmacy after several years in the workforce.'

Was he legit? Mia had no way of knowing.

'Sydney born, bred and educated. Alice is my only sibling. Our parents died in a plane crash when I was in my teens. I gained training in specialist cosmetology, dated, became engaged to a doctor.' The next part was painful. 'I wanted the sex to wait until our wedding night.' She effected a seemingly faint shrug. 'He agreed, but took his pleasure elsewhere. I found out, we split, and I enrolled in a Brisbane university.' Her life, encapsulated in a three-minute time-frame. 'You?'

The coffee was how he liked it, strong, black and sweet.

He searched Mia's features, glimpsed the faint edge of emotional damage and tamped down anger at the man who'd caused it.

'Born in Perth of Greek heritage, educated in Sydney, spent two years in New York, two in Athens. Returned to Sydney when my father and grandfather were killed in a car accident.'

'You left out the women,' she said solemnly.

His dark eyes held faint humour. 'You expect me to say there were many, when they number far fewer than you imagine.'

She met and held his steady gaze. 'I guess it depends on the individual interpretation of *few*.'

Mia finished her tea, and sought to end the evening. 'It's getting late.'

Nikolos extracted a note and slid it beneath his cup to cover the bill, then he stood up and led the way to his car.

'How do you feel about dinner Saturday night?'

'Another date? So soon?'

He deactivated the locking mechanism, opened the passenger door and waited until she was seated before crossing round to slip behind the wheel.

'Call it a briefing in preparation for Sunday lunch with Angelena and Sofia.'

Oh, hell, for a moment she'd forgotten the official family conference. 'Will Cris be there?'

The car eased into the flow of traffic, gained speed, only to pause at a set of lights.

'You want Cris to return the favour of ally?'

Mia was suddenly alert to his tone, and she momentarily froze. Nikolos couldn't know...

'Did you think I was unaware of my brother's sexual proclivity?'

She felt as if she were skating on thin ice. What did she say? Hell, what *could* she say? 'Cris is a friend.'

'Your loyalty to him is commendable.'

Mia searched his features, and caught very little of his expression in the dim interior of the car. 'He's a nice guy.'

'Yes, he is, and I'll do everything in my power to protect him.'

Relief eased the tension, and she offered quietly, 'Perhaps you should tell him that.'

'I already have.'

But what of the Karedes women? 'Your mother and grandmother?' Mia queried cautiously.

'It's Cris' choice to confide in Sofia when he's ready.'

It came as a surprise when Nikolos drew the Mercedes to a halt at the kerb outside Alice's home.

'I've acquainted them with the truth of my involvement with you.'

Oh, *nice* one! '*Thanks*. So now I'm a slut for having sex within hours of meeting you.'

'No.'

'What do you mean...*no*?'

Did she have any idea how magnificent she was when battling anger? Her eyes glowed with it, and her body tensed as tight as a finely tuned bow.

She brought out the most incredible instincts in him. Instincts he hadn't known he possessed.

'They trust my judgement.' His slightly accented drawl held a tinge of humour, which served to incense her.

'Really?' She lifted a hand and clicked her fingers. She was on a roll, and couldn't stop. 'Just like that?'

'They have no reason to disbelieve me.'

Mia didn't attempt to hide her scepticism. 'You think not?'

Mia summoned a mental image of Angelena Karedes, and gritted her teeth. Enduring Sunday lunch was going to be as tricky as attempting to walk through a minefield!

'You'll be treated with dignity and respect.'

On the surface. But what of the hidden undercurrents?

Mia released her seat belt and reached for the door-clasp.

'You forgot something.'

She turned towards him in puzzlement.

'This.' Nikolos captured her head in both hands and lowered his mouth to hers in a kiss that tore her composure to shreds.

It would be so easy to invite more, to touch him as she wanted him to touch her. Attempt in some way to ease the ache deep inside.

Except it wouldn't be enough, for either of them.

His lips trailed to her temple, then explored a delicate cheekbone before settling at the edge of her mouth.

'I—please,' she said in a desperate voice. She couldn't stay. Daredn't.

Nikolos stifled a husky groan as he traced the soft curve of her mouth with his lips, felt their faint quiver as she sought control, and sank in for an evocative tasting.

'Go,' he bade gently as he relinquished her. 'I'll call you when I've confirmed a booking for Saturday evening.'

Mia unlatched the door and slid from the passenger seat without so much as a backward glance.

It took mere seconds to reach Alice's front door, insert the key, then close it behind. With a defeated movement she leant back against it and closed her eyes.

Dear heaven.

She was filled with the taste and feel of him, every sensory nerve-end *alive* with deep, aching need.

For twelve weeks she'd schooled herself to accept a certain rationale, employing logic and reason to her inexplicable behaviour on that fateful night.

There were the vivid dreams as her subconscious forced her to relive the cataclysmic assault he'd had on her senses. And her willing participation.

Now that she'd seen him again it was worse, so much worse than she could have ever imagined. For she was caught in a trap, legally bound to allow him access to their child once it was born, and committed to maintaining contact, sharing decisions, *seeing* him on a regular basis.

Any thought she'd entertained of moving on, creating a new life for herself and rearing a child on her own no longer existed.

Nikolos Karedes would find her, wherever she went, whatever she did. He was that sort of man. Possessed of omnipotent power, with sufficient wealth and resources to hunt her down. Worse, he could inevitably use that power to pursue his own ends.

It wasn't fair, Mia railed silently as she moved through the house to the bedroom she occupied.

But then, when was life ever fair?

CHAPTER SIX

SEVERAL hours of intense retail therapy had done much to bring Mia's wardrobe up to date…something that hadn't ranked high on her list of priorities over the past three years, given university apparel mainly comprised jeans, cargo pants, tee shirts, with an added jacket during winter.

The need to discuss how they should handle lunch with Sofia and Angelena seemed reasonable, and Mia wasn't averse to Nikolos' suggestion they talk over dinner.

'Another date with Nikolos?' Matt teased as Mia entered the lounge minutes ahead of the time Nikolos specified he'd be there.

'It's not a date,' Mia explained, and incurred a boyish grin.

'Looks like a date to me.'

She rolled her eyes in mild exasperation. 'You want me to take you horse-riding in the morning?'

'Okay, so it's not a date.'

'Thank you.'

'Stop it, you two,' Alice admonished with a laugh, and gave Mia her full attention. 'You look gorgeous.'

There was something about a basic black dress, faultless make-up, and minimum jewellery. Black stiletto heeled pumps, a stylish evening purse...

'Seriously gorgeous,' Matt endorsed, wriggling his eyebrows in mock admiration.

'You're a menace,' Mia accorded with affectionate indulgence. 'Fast forward ten years, and heaven help the female population.'

'*Ten?* I was thinking maybe five.'

'Try seven, minimum, or you're jail-bait.'

'Threats, promises, and blackmail?'

It was difficult to contain her laughter. 'All three, and more,' she declared. 'And what your loving mother doesn't finish, I will.'

'Two women ruling my life,' Matt declared, throwing his hands up in mock despair. 'What guy has *two*?'

Mia tilted his chin and planted a kiss on his forehead. 'You do, and don't you forget it!'

'Car just pulled up.'

Levity fled in a second, and was replaced by nervous tension. Did nerve-ends fray? Or stretch to breaking point? Hers felt as if they did both, simultaneously.

How was it possible to experience such a conflicting mixture of emotions? It didn't make sense.

But then, nothing had made sense from the first moment she'd set eyes on Nikolos Karedes.

All she had to do was look at him as he preceded Alice into the room, and everything else faded from her vision, her mind.

His tall, broad frame bore superb tailoring. Armani? Fine blue cotton shirt, silk tie several shades darker, hand-stitched shoes.

'Hi.' Even to her own ears, her greeting sounded incredibly banal.

Nikolos inclined his head. 'Hello.' He turned towards Matt. 'Hi there.' His mouth curved to form a wide smile as he quizzed, 'Is that warpaint?'

Recognition was instantaneous as he used a hand to scrub the lipstick from his forehead, explaining, 'Mia kissed me.'

'Lucky fellow.'

Nikolos' voice held a teasing drawl that did strange things to her composure. Did he realise the effect he had on her? Probably. In fact, she was sure of it!

'Shall we leave?' she managed coolly in a determined bid to exert some measure of control.

'Have fun,' Matt offered innocuously minutes later as Mia followed Nikolos to the car.

The restaurant he'd chosen was situated in one of the inner city suburbs, and intimately small. The sort of place where bookings were made weeks in advance.

'The chef is a personal friend,' Nikolos relayed on being greeted with affection and ushered to what had to be the best table in the house.

'Fine food, wine and exemplary service,' Mia accorded lightly.

He wanted to reach out a hand and trail his fingers down her cheek, cup her chin and outline the curve of her mouth with his thumb.

Except she'd probably bite him if he did.

The thought amused him, and for a moment he was seriously tempted just for the hell of it. Except it might lead to her walking away from the table, out of the restaurant, and hailing the first cab that passed.

She really was something else, he mused as he pretended interest in the wine list. There was no coquetry, no false smiles or attempt at seduction. What was more, she didn't appear to give a *jot* for his wealth or social position.

She possessed beauty that came from within. It was evident in her smile, the teasing gleam apparent in those liquid brown eyes whenever she was with her sister and nephew.

For the time-span of one night...a total of too few hours, she'd plumbed the emotional depths and gifted him everything she was, all she could be, and more.

He wanted back what they'd shared. Dammit, most of all he needed *her*. Beneath him, over him. Innocently generous, eager to please, and passionately genuine in her ecstatic reaction to every pleasure he chose to bestow.

Since when had *want* become *need*?

Mia chose a non-alcoholic spritzer, ordered a starter and a main course, then settled back in her chair. An hour and a half, two hours at the most, and they should have reached comparable tactics.

She picked up her goblet and sipped the cool drink, then set it back down. 'I imagine you've given tomorrow's game plan some thought?'

'Angelena and Sofia are aware of the facts, and that any decisions made will be our own.'

'But?' Mia queried bluntly.

'They offered a few suggestions.'

'I hardly dare ask.'

The waiter delivered their starter, checked Nikolos' wine goblet, then quietly retreated.

'Relatively, they mirror my own.'

Mia forked a delicate morsel from her plate and savoured it. 'So we have an impasse.'

'Not entirely.' His voice was deceptively mild, and she carefully replaced her fork.

'Go on.'

'You could marry me.'

'Excuse me?'

'Marriage,' Nikolos reiterated with hateful ease. 'Consider the benefits as opposed to sharing the child between two parents in different residences.'

'You're insane.'

'Am I?'

'You base what is meant to be a whole-of-life decision on one night of good sex?' *Good* didn't come close.

'Our sexual compatibility is a bonus.'

'No,' she said steadily.

'You don't agree it's a bonus?'

'No, I won't marry you.' He could give her everything she could ever want or need. A lifestyle almost without equal.

'Would you care to give me a reason why not?'

'I'd always know it was a choice you felt impelled to make.'

'You're so sure of that?'

How could it be anything else? 'Yes,' she said simply.

'What if you're wrong?'

'I had the textbook engagement,' she reiterated quietly. 'Friends for two years, engaged for one. As it turned out, I hardly knew him at all.'

'So come live with me.'

Her eyes widened. 'I beg your pardon?'

'Move in with me, share my life, and determine whether marriage to me would be so abhorrent.'

'I don't think that's a good idea.'

'Afraid, Mia?'

'Of course not.' And knew she lied. If she went with him she'd never want to leave. And that was a luxury she couldn't afford.

While some women might eagerly settle for material possessions and social prestige in exchange for sexual favours, she wasn't one of them. Nor could she accept or condone a string of affairs in an open marriage.

'So what do you have to lose?'

You can't begin to know! she thought. To exist in a relationship where she knew she didn't have his heart and soul would only be half a life, and one she'd rather not have at all.

'I'm Alice's guest for the summer vacation.'

'That isn't a problem.'

Mia raised one eyebrow. 'Really?' She waited until the waiter cleared their plates before continuing, 'So I get to visit Alice and Matt whenever I'm not at work, socialising, or sleeping with you. Is that how you envisage such an arrangement?'

Nikolos' eyes narrowed. 'It isn't my intention to impose any restrictions on when and where you spend time with your sister.'

'Except you'd expect to take priority.' She examined the contents of her goblet, then speared his gaze with her own. 'Tell me, do you always get your own way?'

'Mostly.' He leaned back in his chair and regarded her carefully. She was something else...vibrant, sassy, and far too independent for his peace of mind.

'Perhaps you should make me aware of Angelena and Sofia's *suggestions*?'

'In order to be prepared?'

'I imagine your mother will be politely circumspect in comparison to Angelena.'

Nikolos' husky laughter sent sensation slithering down her spine. Worse, she appeared to have a host of butterflies in her stomach fluttering their wings madly in an attempt to escape. Neither was a comfortable feeling.

'*Yiayia* is adamant a Karedes heir should be born within the legitimate bounds of marriage,' he drawled, and Mia rolled her eyes in expressive dismissal.

'No exception acceptable.'

'None,' he agreed. 'Sofia suggests the announcement of an immediate engagement, followed by marriage in the foreseeable future.'

'Before the child's birth.'

'Preferably.'

She looked at him carefully. 'You're prepared to go along with that?'

'Would I suggest it if not?'

Doubtful. He wasn't a man to be coerced into anything, much less marriage. 'So tomorrow I stand alone against the three of you?'

Nikolos regarded her thoughtfully. 'Are you going to renege on lunch?'

And appear a wimp? 'No.'

The edges of his mouth twitched with musing humour as the waiter presented their main meal. 'I'm pleased to hear it.'

Tomorrow's confrontation held all the connotations of being a familial battle. One any sane person would go to any lengths to avoid.

Mia looked at the food displayed on her plate with artistic flair, and wondered if she'd be able to do it justice, for her appetite seemed to have fled.

Worse, her stomach appeared to be on the verge of a revolt. Morning sickness? In the evening? *Now?* The powder room was *where?*

There was barely time to utter 'excuse me' as she leapt from her chair and made a dignified dash to the designated powder room.

Minutes later she took a deep breath and placed a hand to her stomach. Everything seemed fine, but maybe she should give it another minute or two before venturing back to the table.

Mia glanced up as the door swung open, and she gave an involuntary gasp as she saw Nikolos in the aperture. 'You can't come in here.'

'Watch me.' His eyes narrowed as he raked her slender frame. Her features were pale, and her eyes seemed too large for her face. 'Are you okay?'

'I'm fine.' She smoothed a hand over her hair. 'Let's get back to the table.' She managed a faint smile. 'A cup of tea would go down well.'

He arranged it with considerable speed, and she sipped the brew appreciatively, feeling better with each passing minute.

'Nikolos.' The voice was feminine and familiar. 'Who would have thought to find you here?'

Mia didn't need to turn in her chair to determine just who was standing close by.

'Anouska.'

Coincidence? Maybe. Or perhaps Anouska, aware of Nikolos' favoured eating places, could have phoned to check if he had a booking here tonight.

Mia moved slightly and murmured a polite greeting, noting the silk evening trouser suit, the jewellery, and superbly applied make-up. The fashionista looked a million dollars, and was very aware of the fact.

Mia was reminded of a preening peacock, aware she had the gender wrong. A peahen was utterly plain.

Anouska's male companion was too smooth, his smile too practised. Artificial superficiality was alive and well.

'We have a reservation, but perhaps we could join you?'

Great. Just what she needed. Another round with Anouska vying for one-upwomanship.

'We were just leaving.'

They were? He'd barely finished his main meal, and, even if he intended passing on dessert, he had yet to order coffee.

Was he doing this for her benefit? Or because he chose not to handle Anouska's company?

Whatever the reason, Mia felt a certain gratitude as Nikolos beckoned the waiter and requested their bill.

'If you'll excuse us?'

Anouska's pout was pure Hollywood. 'Shame, darling. We could have had some fun.'

It depended on one's definition of *fun*, Mia determined as she rose to her feet and offered a polite 'goodnight'.

In the car, she sat in silence observing the passing night scenery, the bright neon advertising signs, the traffic.

'Nothing to say?'

Nikolos' drawling voice held a tinge of humour, and she turned towards him, aware of his profile in the semi darkness of the car's interior. A profile that assumed angles and planes beneath the illumination of oncoming headlights.

'What would you have me say?' Mia countered lightly.

'Anouska doesn't want to give you up? Thanks for a lovely meal? How about, Please take me home?'

His soft laughter sounded impossibly husky in the close confines of the car.

'Thanks,' Mia added quietly, and incurred his sharp glance. 'For making a quick exit.'

'How are you feeling?'

Don't sound as if you care. The thought that he might almost brought her undone. 'Fine,' she managed evenly. Physically, she accorded silently. Emotionally was something else.

Alice's house was in darkness with only the outside light burning when Nikolos brought the car to a smooth halt at the kerb.

'I'll see you tomorrow,' Mia indicated as she reached for the door-clasp.

He leaned towards her and trailed light fingers across her cheek. 'Midday. I'll collect you.' He traced her lower lip with his thumb-pad, felt its slight tremble beneath his touch, then sank back in his seat. 'Sleep well.'

Mia slid out from the passenger seat and crossed the path to her sister's home. Seconds later Nikolos' car purred to life as she closed the door quietly behind her.

Mia rose early and drove Matt to his horse-riding lesson, commended his skills, and returned in time for a late breakfast, after which Alice left with Matt for a day at the beach, offering a humorous last-minute instruction.

'Don't let the dragon ladies win.'

'Slay 'em,' was Matt's throwaway directive, accompanied by a figuratively graphic sword thrust-and-parry movement.

'Your talent should be displayed on the stage,' Mia responded in a droll voice, and laughed when he wriggled his eyebrows expressively.

'You think?'

'Go,' she begged. 'I need peace and quiet in which to plan my modus operandi.'

'You'd have more fun with us at the beach,' Matt declared. 'You could bring Nikolos.'

Now there was a thought... 'Maybe another time,' she said lightly. 'Today I have to do the grown-up thing.'

'Serious stuff, huh?'

You can't begin to believe how serious! 'You could say that.'

'Good luck.'

Her smile was heartfelt. 'Thanks.'

It was relatively early, and she put a load of washing into the machine, tidied the kitchen and did some household chores.

Tomorrow she was due to begin work at the pharmacy, and she checked her student identification tag, organised her uniform, then hit the shower.

What did one wear when going into battle? Mia mused as she checked through her clothes.

Lunch with the Karedes matriarchs loomed like a spectre before her, and she chose a sleeveless silk dress in jade green with a wide scooped neckline, and a bias-cut skirt.

It was stylish in design, feminine, and provided a sophisticated image.

Make-up was cleverly understated with emphasis on her eyes, and she wore her hair in a smooth French twist, added minimum jewellery, then slid her feet into stilettos.

She checked her watch, then caught up her clutch purse and walked through to the lounge in time to see Nikolos' car pull into the driveway.

Mia drew in a deep breath and released it, then opened the door.

Party time.

Well, almost, she amended as she locked up and turned to meet Nikolos, whose height and breadth of shoulder seemed vaguely intimidating this close. Or maybe she was just acutely aware of him at a base level, knowing how it felt to be enfolded against that hard-muscled chest...and in need of being offered such a sanctuary again, for comfort and re-assurance.

Oh, for heaven's sake, get a grip!

'Hi.' She caught his smile and offered one of her own.

'How are you?'

'Fine,' Mia admitted honestly. 'Apart from feeling as if I'm about to enter the lions' den.'

His mouth curved with humour. 'I won't let them eat you.'

'Ah, you'll parry verbal swords for me?'

'Count on it.'

She effected a slight mock curtsy. 'My knight in shining armour.'

Nikolos' eyes gleamed as he caught hold of her hand and brought it to his lips. 'My pleasure.'

The gesture quickened her pulse and sent warmth flooding her veins. A fact she managed to disguise by pinning a smile in place and holding it there.

He led the way to the car and saw her seated before crossing round to slip in behind the wheel.

It took a while to reach Vaucluse, and enter the lovely tree-lined avenue where Angelena's stately home was situated.

A gold Lexus stood parked beneath the portico, and Nikolos parked beside it.

'Ready?'

Her eyes met and held his. 'Let's go do this, shall we?'

They were greeted at the front door by a manservant and ushered indoors. Mia was aware of a large foyer, panelled walls, oil paintings and antique furniture as Nikolos led her into a formal lounge where Angelena and Sofia were seated in separate chairs.

'Nikolos,' Angelena acknowledged, and inclined her head towards Mia. 'Mia.'

'*Yiayia*. Mother.'

Formality was obviously the order of the day, with a certain disapproving stiffness that hardly augured well.

Sofia offered a conciliatory smile that was perhaps meant to soften Angelena's stance. Although Mia wasn't prepared to bank on it.

'Please,' Angelena began. 'Take a seat and be comfortable.'

Comfort wasn't exactly a word Mia cared to associate with the matriarch. She could conjure up a few that seemed more suitable as she selected a chair, aware Nikolos chose to remain standing.

How long would it be before the purpose of this visit was mentioned? Social drinks first, then straight into the fray? Or did Angelena intend to feed them first?

Drinks, Mia determined minutes later as she accepted a soda.

'Lunch will be served shortly,' Angelena informed. 'After which, we will address the current situation.'

Polite civility at all costs, Mia mused. So she was to be offered food before being met-aphorically fed to the lions? On the grounds she might be more mellow and less prepared? In order to fall in with whatever the matriarch deemed an acceptable resolution?

It was a relief when lunch was announced. A meal where the food was superbly pre-sented and, without doubt, delicious. Although Mia's tastebuds appeared to have gone on strike.

She was supremely conscious of Nikolos seated at her side, aware just how his close proximity was adding to her nervous tension.

'You've hardly eaten a thing,' Sofia noted with apparent concern. 'Would you prefer something else? Some salad, perhaps?'

'I'm fine,' she reassured, knowing it was an extension of the truth. The thought of her stomach going into revolt *here* was the last thing she needed.

'I developed the most unlikely cravings when I was pregnant with Nikolos,' Sofia offered with a faint smile. 'Food I'd never liked suddenly became all I wanted to eat. In weird combinations.'

Mia passed on dessert and chose a selection of fresh fruit.

'We'll have coffee in the lounge,' Angelena declared when her manservant appeared and began clearing the table.

Okay, Mia accorded silently. This is when the fun begins!

Sure enough, the matriarch waited only as long as it took for them to relocate to the lounge and be served coffee and tea before she launched directly into the specific purpose of today's invitation.

'We need to discuss plans.'

Plans? 'There are no plans that I'm aware of,' Mia began, only to incur a long, piercing look meant to diminish her into subservient silence.

'You will, of course, marry.'

The matriarch's tone carried unequivocal conviction, and Mia unconsciously held her breath for a few seconds before she ventured with polite civility, 'I don't see marriage as a prerequisite to having or raising a child.'

'*Yiayia,*' Nikolos admonished gently. 'It is for Mia and I to make a decision.'

The temperature in the room seemed to drop a few degrees as Angelena took pains to compose herself.

'I find it totally unacceptable for a Karedes heir to be born out of wedlock.'

Mia felt as if she'd been suddenly flung back into the previous century. 'I have no intention of denying my child its place within the Karedes family,' she said calmly, 'but I won't be coerced into a marriage I don't want.'

The matriarch's faint indrawn hiss of disapproval was more visible than audible.

'You *do* realise the importance of the Karedes name?'

Mia's chin tilted fractionally. 'More important than the future happiness of a child born into a marriage based on convenience in which both parents find themselves trapped?'

If it were possible for Angelena to draw herself more tightly together, the effort was made. 'My grandson is a wealthy man in his own right, and possesses a generous disposition. You'll lead a fulfilling life, and doubtless bear more children.'

'To further the Karedes dynasty?'

'Of course.' Angelena fixed Nikolos with a dark beady stare. 'You have proposed marriage, I assume?'

'Naturally,' Nikolos drawled with hateful ease. 'Did you imagine I would not?'

'And?' the matriarch demanded imperiously.

Mia didn't wait for him to answer. 'I turned him down.'

The elderly woman's eyes dilated. 'I beg your pardon?'

This was rapidly digressing into a full-scale argument, albeit refined...just.

'You expect me to commit to a man who doesn't love me? Live with him, sleep with him, raise children with him?' She waited a few seconds. 'Look the other way when he takes on a lover or two, or more? Accept and condone his behaviour?'

Haughty didn't begin to describe Angelena's expression.

'You dare accuse Nikolos of such indiscretions?'

Oh, my. 'I don't know Nikolos well enough to judge him.'

'You didn't think of that when you leapt into bed with him.'

'The desire for sex was entirely mutual,' Mia corrected as she held the elderly lady's gaze. 'Last time I heard, consensual sex isn't a crime.'

'*Yiayia,*' Nikolos chastised. 'Enough.'

'I agree,' Sofia declared. 'Let's not make demands. Instead, we should welcome Mia into the family, endorse our support for whatever decision she chooses to make, and resolve to get to know her.'

An ally? The day suddenly became marginally brighter.

'An excellent suggestion,' Nikolos concurred as he placed his cup and saucer onto a nearby table. 'Now, if you'll excuse us? Mia and I have arrangements for the remainder of the day.'

They did?

'You realise I will not let this rest?'

'*Yiayia,*' he warned with dangerous silkiness. 'In this instance, you have no choice.' His voice gentled. 'Try not to concern yourself overmuch, hmm?'

Mia was surprised to see the faint shimmer of tears in the elderly lady's eyes before she blinked them away.

'How can I not?'

It was almost three when they left, and Mia sat in silence as Nikolos eased the powerful car through the gates and turned into the tree-lined avenue.

A number of conflicting thoughts fought for supremacy, some of which she didn't want to face. At least not here, not now.

Was she being a fool to stubbornly refuse contemplating a life with Nikolos? She would be inextricably bound up with him via legal custody rights. Marriage would provide stability in more ways than one, together with the bonus of sharing his bed.

It was impossible to ignore the surge of warmth flooding her veins at the thought of having him reach for her through the night, their shared intimacy and the hundred and one sensual delights their lovemaking would provide.

Sure, a tiny imp taunted. You'd contemplate using good sex as a basis for a lifetime commitment? *Are you mad?*

An elderly woman's tears have led you to give Nikolos' proposal a moment's consideration, when common sense dismisses it out of hand?

What had seemed so clear-cut less than twenty-four hours ago now provided an element of doubt. Minuscule, but there nonetheless.

'I thought we might drive up to the northern beaches.'

Mia turned towards him, aware of his forceful image, the well-defined facial structure that combined with a dramatic mesh of intense sensuality and power.

'We could have dinner, maybe take in a movie,' he continued.

'Dinner,' she agreed. 'I'll take a rain check on the movie. I start work tomorrow.'

'I'll endeavour to return you to Alice's home at a respectable hour.'

Mia detected a degree of musing humour in his voice. 'You're not going to argue with me?'

He offered her a quick glance before returning his attention to the road. 'Would it do any good?'

'No.'

Nikolos activated a CD and soft background music flowed through the sound system. It was relaxing, almost therapeutic, and she wondered if he used it as a de-stressing device.

Entrepreneurial power-broking had to involve decision-making at a high level, maintaining constant touch with directorial and managerial staff, keeping track of every movement within the company.

His physique denoted he took time to work out. Did he follow any sport? Was he a team player or did he prefer a solo activity?

'Ask,' Nikolos drawled as he eased to a halt at a traffic intersection.

'And you'll answer?'

'You have twenty questions in mind?'

'Very funny.'

'Changed your mind?'

'Do you travel often?'

'Frequently. Interstate, overseas.'

'For long periods of time?'

'Most business can be wrapped up in a day or two within Australia.' He effected a faint shrug. 'Overseas, taking flights into the equation...four or five days. Maybe a week. For a few years I rotated almost equally between New York, Athens, Tokyo and Sydney.'

'With no one place to call home?'

'I have apartments in each city.'

She should have guessed. 'Must be easier than living out of a suitcase.'

'Indeed.' But lonely, he could have added. Long flights, an empty apartment at the end of it, a solitary bed...with only the occasional selective exception. Business had become his focus in a bid to prove he was a worthy successor to his late father.

Until recently. One night was all it had taken to make him question his priorities.

One woman.

Who, because of fate and a broken prophylactic, would bear their child.

Would she believe he wanted her in his life? Dammit, *needed* her, as he'd never needed any other woman?

Patience, he instilled silently. He manipu-lated multimillion-dollar deals on a weekly basis. Dealt and went head-to-head with some of the biggest power-brokers in the world. He could handle a petite, sable-haired slip of a woman…couldn't he?

'All those long flights and intense business meetings,' Mia ventured. 'What do you do to keep fit?'

'Martial arts. It combines body and mind, and promotes self-discipline.'

It figured.

They spent a relaxing few hours exploring the northern beaches, and enjoyed delicious seafood in a waterfront restaurant before tak-ing the highway south.

It was almost ten when Nikolos eased the car to a halt outside Alice's home, and Mia offered a polite 'goodnight' as she reached for the door-clasp.

Only to feel his hands close over her shoul-ders as he turned her towards him, then his mouth covered hers in a kiss that literally robbed the breath from her throat.

There was hunger, and so much more... passion that threatened the fragile tenure of her control. She *ached* with it, and became lost in the sensual thrall until there was only him...and deep, throbbing need.

It was Nikolos who broke the contact, easing back gently as she brokenly voiced her regret.

'Go *now*,' he bade huskily. 'Or I take you to my apartment. Choose.'

Oh, God. As if there was a choice! Yet there was only one she could make. 'I can't,' Mia whispered, and knew she lied. It would be so easy to go with him. So very easy.

'Then go, Mia.'

She did, quickly slipping from the passenger seat in a bid to put distance between them. Otherwise she'd give in to temptation and throw self-caution to the wind.

She didn't look back as she walked swiftly to the door, and inside she made straight to her bedroom where she leaned back against the closed door for an age, until her rapid breathing steadied, and the heightened tension began to lessen.

Then she slowly removed her clothes, cleansed off her make-up, and slid between the sheets to lie staring at the darkened ceiling until sleep took her captive.

CHAPTER SEVEN

THERE was something intensely satisfying about being in the workforce and employing theory with day-to-day practice. It was an ongoing learning experience that Mia enjoyed, especially the interaction with customers requiring information about prescription and over-the-counter medications.

The head pharmacist proved courteous, and helpful with each of her enquiries, his manager likewise, and the staff were friendly.

The customers were a mixed group of people of varying ages and nationalities, some extremely colourful, others quiet, even diffident.

Careful shoppers, some elderly and visibly frail for whom Mia felt oddly protective. Brash young teenagers who swaggered in, wearing fashionably tattered jeans, designer tee shirts, shades and sporting various body piercings.

There were also the less favourable customers on methadone programmes, and the addicts who came in for their sealed packs of needles.

The young girls who wanted to fill in time by sampling perfumes, cosmetics, trying out lipsticks, requiring advice on blushers and mascara, and the dreaded acne.

It made for an interesting and varied day, and she emerged from the pharmacy at quitting time to find Nikolos standing indolently at ease on the pavement.

'What are you doing here?' The words slipped out before she gave them much thought.

'Whatever happened to *hello*?'

His musing drawl brought a tinge of soft colour to her cheeks. 'I didn't expect to see you,' she managed evenly.

'I thought you might appreciate a ride home.'

'Taking care of the Karedes heir?'

His eyes narrowed. 'I'll let that pass.'

'Kind of you.'

He indicated the Mercedes parked at the kerb. 'You want to argue?'

'I feel I should, just for the hell of it.'

'Maybe you could compromise?'

'As long as you don't intend making a habit of playing chauffeur.'

'Get in, Mia.'

It was easier to comply, and seated inside the luxury vehicle she had to question her sanity. Hormones, she decided as Nikolos slid in behind the wheel and drove her the short distance to Alice's home.

'I could have walked.'

'Is that a token objection, or an attempt to argue?'

She cast him a steady look. 'Oh, why don't I go for broke, and admit to both?'

'Let me get you home, then you can change and I'll feed you.'

'Excuse me?'

'We'll go have dinner somewhere.'

'You can go have dinner. I want a shower, food, and an early night.'

'You can have that. I'll even throw in a foot massage.'

She closed her eyes at the thought of such bliss, then opened them again in time to see him pull in to the kerb outside Alice's home.

Behind a four-wheel drive. A very shiny, new-looking Mercedes four-wheel drive.

Alice had a visitor?

'Yours,' Nikolos elaborated, indicating the vehicle.

'No,' Mia said firmly.

'I insist.'

'I don't need transport.'

He handed over a set of keys. 'Consider it a gift. Indulge me.'

'Why?'

'Because I'll sleep easier.'

'That's a valid reason?'

'It is to me.' He dropped the keys into her lap. 'Now let's go inside, shall we?'

'Alice will have already organised dinner.'

'I don't imagine she'll mind if you give it a miss.'

Alice didn't mind at all. So much for sibling loyalty! Although that wasn't strictly fair, Mia decided as she hit the shower. Alice wanted whatever was best for her.

Designer jeans, a jacket over a vest top, low-heeled sandals, just a touch of make-up, and she was ready.

Nikolos chose a small Italian restaurant only a few kilometres distant, where the redolent aroma of pasta sauce set the digestive juices flowing. Bruschetta, a small plate of delicious tortellini was *perfetto*, combined with light background music…it teased the senses, calmed and lifted them.

The service was warm and friendly, the atmosphere, with its small tables dressed in red and white checked gingham, empty Chianti bottles with their candles…

It was charming.

'Thank you.' Mia forked the last mouthful, then pressed the napkin to her lips.

'For?'

'Bringing me here,' she said simply, and watched his mouth curve into a musing smile.

'My pleasure.' He leaned back in his chair. 'How was your first day?'

'Interesting.'

One eyebrow lifted. 'That's it? The entire day encapsulated into one word?'

'The elderly like to chat. Mothers with young children want quick service, and teenage girls spend time trying out the make-up testers.'

The waiter cleared away their plates, and asked if they'd like to see the dessert menu.

'Not for me.'

Nikolos ordered tea, and coffee for himself.

'I imagine you spent the day wheeling and dealing, meetings, phone calls.'

He reflected on one particular problem and the fact it required his personal attention. 'I fly out to New York on the late-evening flight.'

She looked at him more closely, and glimpsed the fine edge of tension. Fine lines fanned out from the corner of his eyes, and there was a brooding quality apparent she couldn't define. 'I take it this wasn't factored into your schedule?'

'No.'

'How long will it take?'

'Four, five days.'

Their tea and coffee arrived, and he took his black with sugar. 'We have an invitation to attend a pre-Christmas party on Saturday evening.'

'*We* do?'

The corner of his mouth lifted at her emphasis. 'Yes. Are you going to object?'

'Will it make any difference?'

'I intend to make an appearance. I'd prefer to have you join me.'

Mia offered him a solemn smile. 'In that case, I accept.'

He drained the rest of his coffee as she sipped the remainder of her tea. 'Shall we leave?' He signalled for the bill, paid when it came, then he led her out to the car.

'Thanks,' she offered quietly when he drew in to the kerb outside Alice's home. 'I hope everything goes well in New York.' She reached for the door-clasp, only for his hand to close over hers.

'Not so fast.'

'Nikolos—' Whatever else she might have said remained locked in her throat as his mouth possessed hers in a kiss that tore her composure to shreds.

Hard, passionate, it swept her towards a place she badly wanted to be, and her hands crept up to link together behind his head as he deepened the kiss.

It wasn't enough, and she was hardly aware of the faint despairing groan that sounded low in her throat as he began to withdraw. Slowly, and with infinite care, un-

til his lips, his tongue, soothed instead of ignited her senses.

Then she was free as he lifted his head,
and her eyes were wide luminous pools as
she looked at him.

Nikolos brushed gentle fingers down her
cheek, then bent and trailed his mouth gently
over her own.

'I'll call you.'

Mia wasn't capable of uttering a word, and
she simply nodded, then she opened the door,
slid out, and stood watching as he cleared the
driveway and accelerated down the street.

'What do you think about having a barbecue
on Sunday?' Alice queried next morning as
she checked the time, then drained the last of
her coffee. 'Just a few close friends. Ask
Nikolos when he phones.'

Casual outdoor eating held a definite ap-
peal. 'Sounds great.'

'Five minutes, Matt,' Alice reminded
as she headed towards the hall to fix her
make-up.

'Maybe you could drop me to school,' Matt suggested wistfully. 'Just a small detour on your way to work?'

Mia tilted her head as she regarded him across the breakfast table. 'Tonight after dinner we'll take the four-wheel drive for a test spin. Okay?'

He punched a fist high in the air. *'Yes.'*

Mia left the house a short while later. It was a lovely summer's day, the sky clear with scarcely a drift of cloud, and she cast the four-wheel drive a glance, admired its solid lines, the shiny paintwork, and walked right on past.

Walking was good, she assured silently. Stubborn single-mindedness had nothing to do with her decision…and knew she fooled no one.

The morning passed quickly, and she took an early lunch break, choosing to eat a healthy chicken salad sandwich in a nearby park. Bottled water, a magazine, a comfortable bench beneath a shady wide-branched tree…what more could anyone ask?

The gardens were lovely, with splendid stands of strelitzia providing colour, adding to an array of native plants, and in the distance a jacaranda in full bloom casting a carpet of pale lilac petals beneath its branches.

There were birds perching high, undisturbed by the sounds of traffic and human habitation, and their calls held a pleasant melodic quality.

'Enjoying your lunch?'

Mia glanced up from the magazine and her eyes widened at the sight of Anouska standing a few feet distant.

Chance was a fine thing, but having the fashionista appear here, now, was stretching coincidence too far.

Which meant Anouska had elicited information from a source…the question was *who*? Alice was a definite no. Nikolos? Doubtful.

'Anouska.' Cool, calm and collected. She could do all three. 'Just passing through?' As if.

How difficult would it be to determine the suburb where Alice lived and phone a few pharmacies in the area? Would a temporary staff member's name be confirmed?

Depending on the basis for such a query, it was possible.

'I doubt you're that naive.'

'Nikolos.' As if there was any doubt.

Anouska examined her flawlessly polished nails. 'I like a girl who gets to the point.'

Mia made a study of checking her watch. 'Can you wrap it up in five?'

'Darling, I can do it in less.' She flashed a brilliant artificial smile, then honed in for the kill. 'I shall suggest Nikolos insists on DNA. I've no objection if he supports your child. It's just that I intend to have his ring on my finger.'

Mia held the fashionista's pseudo gaze. 'By fair means...or foul?'

'I see we understand each other.'

Mia stood up. 'If you're done, I really have to get back to work.'

'Watch your step.'

'Ditto, Anouska. In spades,' she added as she turned and took the path to the roadside. Within minutes she entered the pharmacy, took time to freshen up, then she resumed work. Rattled, but not shaken, she assured with an attempt at silent humour.

Anouska's threat was almost a joke, except she had the feeling the fashionista was deadly serious.

Why Nikolos? Surely there were other men among the social élite who were rich, attractive and eligible?

Or was Anouska delusional? Fixated on an emotional tie that no longer existed. If it ever had.

The park scene replayed itself over several times during the course of the afternoon, and it was a relief when closing time came.

The walk home cleared her mind, and Matt's welcoming grin, his enthusiasm for a ride in the four-wheel drive swept aside Mia's lingering concern as they discussed their respective days over dinner, then, dishes cleared, she retrieved the set of keys and led the way out to the vehicle.

It was a dream to drive, so smooth and comfortable.

'Wow,' Matt accorded as she headed towards French's Forest, then she headed down to the Spit, found a parking space close to an ice-cream parlour and bought them each a luscious sundae.

They didn't linger long, as Matt had a homework assignment to complete before bedtime.

'I want one of these when I'm old enough to drive,' Matt said with fervour as Mia brought the vehicle to a halt some time later.

'Dream big, study hard, and maybe,' Alice said affectionately as they went indoors.

'Yeah, I know,' he said with boyish enthusiasm. 'One day.'

Mia contemplated sharing Anouska's surprise appearance with Alice as they sipped hot tea while viewing a favourite comedy on one of the television channels.

Then the moment was gone, and it wasn't until she lay in bed that it returned to haunt her. Tomorrow, she decided on the edge of sleep.

Except there was a power cut through the night, and the alarm didn't go off. Consequently they woke later than usual and everything became a mad rush to get out of the house on time.

The day didn't get any better. One of the pharmacy staff called in sick, a truculent child ran amok and emptied an entire shelf of its contents, and an indignant customer insisted Mia had sold him the wrong over-the-counter cough medicine, when she knew she hadn't served him at all.

Mistaken identity? However, retail policy favoured the customer, and he was sufficiently appeased with her apology together with a bottle of the 'correct' medicine.

Mid-afternoon a florist-emblazoned box was delivered with her name on it. Inside were two dozen roses in delicate peach, cream and apricot, and a card bearing *Nikolos*. She sent him a text message, thanking him.

His image rose to the fore, strong, powerful, and a force all on his own. It was easy to recall how it felt to have his mouth possess hers, the touch of his hands on her body...the deep, all-consuming passion he aroused in her without any effort at all.

She could understand Anouska wanting him. What woman wouldn't? Except the emotional aspect of a relationship needed to be equal, and obsessive behaviour shouldn't enter the equation.

Which led her to wonder how far the fashionista would go.

Mia didn't have long to find out. Next morning when Alice left for work she noticed the four-wheel drive had two flat tyres.

'It was fine last night.' A perplexed frown creased her forehead as Matt crouched down for a close inspection.

'One could be a puncture,' Alice offered, and shook her head doubtfully. 'But *two*, both kerbside?'

'I'll have to call a tyre shop and organise for replacements.' She checked the time. 'Go, or you'll be late. I'll ring you during my lunch break.'

'Check my business card file by the phone. You'll find a contact number there.'

She did, and made the call, then she set a brisk walking pace to the pharmacy.

It was late morning when she managed to check with the tyre firm, and it didn't help to learn both tyres had been punctured with a sharp object.

'Intentionally?'

'Yeah, without doubt. You need new ones.'

She wrangled a little on price, gained a discount, and arranged for two new tyres to be fitted.

Lunch was an egg and salad sandwich eaten at a nearby café, where she made the call to Alice from her cellphone.

'Craig Mitchell,' a deep masculine voice answered.

'Mia Fredrickson, Alice's sister.'

'I remember. We met at the gallery exhibition last week,' he acknowledged warmly. 'Alice has just stepped out to retrieve a file for me. Shall I have her call you?'

'Please, my cellphone number.' She made a spur of the moment decision. 'Are you free around midday on Sunday? Alice and I are planning a barbecue lunch for a few friends. It's very informal. We'd like to have you join us.'

'Thank you. Can I contribute anything?'

Mia effected a silent *yes* following his acceptance. 'Just yourself. You have the address?'

'It's on file.'

'We'll look forward to seeing you.'

She cut the call, and sipped her cool drink, assuring herself it wasn't matchmaking as such...merely giving fate a helping hand.

Not that Alice would consider it that, she mused as she flipped through a magazine and waited for her sister to return the call.

When it came she steeled herself for exasperation, maybe irritation...and found herself on the receiving end of both.

'Just what do you think you're doing?'

Here we go...'Craig? The barbecue?'

'Yes!'

'You object?'

'You could have run it by me first.'

'And given you the opportunity to find any number of reasons why Craig shouldn't be invited?'

'I prefer to keep my professional and private lives separate.'

'It's only a barbecue, with a few friends.'

'And Matt,' Alice said heavily. 'Had you thought how it might affect him, having a strange man turn up at the house?'

'Craig is your boss, for heaven's sake.'

'He's also someone Matt has never met. You know I haven't dated since David walked out.'

Instead, her sister had thrown herself into being both parents rolled into one.

'Maybe it's time you did,' Mia offered gently. 'And I'm sorry you think it's such a big deal.'

She recalled only too well how Matt had reacted with Nikolos on the cruiser. The tinge of colour in her sister's cheeks when Craig Mitchell had made an appearance at the gallery...and the warmth apparent in the man's eyes when they had rested on Alice.

'You don't understand.'

'You can handle what you feel for Craig while it remains a professional relationship,' Mia relayed, 'but you're not at all sure how you'll deal with him if it becomes personal?'

'Something like that. Did you organise new tyres?'

'Yes.' Her mouth curved at the edges with the sudden change in their conversation, and took another direction, suggesting, 'Do you feel like taking Matt out for fish and chips tonight? My treat.'

'I should cook—'

'Why? You cook most nights.' Every night. 'Let's pick up fast food and go eat it down by the waterfront. Out of packets,' she added for good measure.

'I know why Matt relishes you holidaying with us,' Alice said with mock severity, and Mia laughed.

'Fast finger food, no plates, no cutlery. Shock, horror.'

'Okay, we'll do it. I'll see you at home.'

The sun still retained much of its warmth as Mia left the pharmacy at the close of the business day.

Her mind strayed to Alice, and she thought how nice it would be for her sister to have a man in her life again. She deserved someone who would protect and care for her, and welcome Matt as his own.

Alice's husband had been a manipulative chameleon whose worst side had appeared soon after the ink had dried on the marriage certificate. Becoming a father hadn't been on his agenda, and Alice had come home from work one day to find the house had been completely emptied. A messy divorce had followed.

A faint sound caught her attention, she saw a blur of movement, then hard hands grabbed her shoulders and attempted to push her to the ground.

Mia went with the momentum, carrying her attacker's body in an arc that put him flat on his back. He lashed out with his foot and connected with her ribs, an action which gained him an essential few seconds to scramble out of reach and get to his feet.

He was young, lean, and identification was impossible...he was wearing a ski-mask.

He motioned for her shoulder-bag, and when she didn't comply he made a grab for it.

Anyone with any sense would have simply handed it over, but she was angry...*really* angry. She clenched both hands together and aimed a hard upward thrust to his jaw, heard his howl of pain, and watched him turn and run.

Martial arts training had finally paid off. And she still had her bag, with most of her dignity intact. Except for a bruised rib or two, she was fine.

'You okay, miss?'

A young kid on a bike wheeled up to her and braked hard, swinging the rear wheel round with a flourish. 'I saw that guy. Want me to chase him?'

Hell, no. 'Don't,' she cautioned. 'He's long gone.'

'I'll walk you home in case he comes back. You're staying at Matt's house, aren't you?'

She hated to squash the youngster's sense of chivalry. 'Yes, I am. And thanks, it's kind of you.'

'No problem.'

Five minutes later he walked her up to Alice's front door, rang the bell, despite Mia assuring him she had a key, and when Alice opened the door he relayed the story with all the importance of a young police cadet.

Matt raced out, and a kind of organised pandemonium followed with Alice insistent on a hospital check-up.

Minutes later Mia found herself bundled into Alice's car with Matt in the rear seat, and each and every one of her protests ignored.

It took a while, between an examination, an ultrasound, before she was given a medical all-clear. The foetus was fine, and she had two bruised ribs.

She turned towards Matt as she slid into the passenger seat. 'I'm hungry, champ. How about you?'

He offered an infectious grin. 'Starving.'

'Okay, so we get to take fish and chips home.'

'I don't think—' Alice began, only to have Mia interrupt.

'We need to eat. Why not make it easy and fun?'

'Fun and easy is cool,' her nephew endorsed.

'Matt—'

Half an hour later they arrived home with individual steaming packets, which they ate as finger food at the dining-room table.

'I think I'll go take a shower,' Mia indicated. Her ribs were giving her hell, and she refused to take anything to relieve the pain. 'Shan't be long.'

She was back in ten minutes, clad in a comfortable cotton nightshirt and a light cotton robe, her face free of make-up and her hair tied back in a pony-tail.

Mia took one look at Alice's stern expression and Matt's crestfallen features. 'What's up?'

'Nikolos rang. I told him about your accident, and hospital,' Matt relayed. 'Mum said I shouldn't have.'

Alice lifted a hand and let it fall again, concern clouding her eyes. 'I took the phone from him, but it was too late.'

'I'm sorry,' Matt said with a seriousness beyond his years. 'I forgot Nikolos was away, and he might worry about you.'

'I told him you were fine,' Alice added quickly. 'He's ringing back.' At that moment the phone rang. 'I guess you'd better answer it.' She turned towards her son. 'Go take a shower, Matt.'

Mia crossed the room and picked up. 'Hi.'

'Nikolos.' His voice sounded deep, and, unless she was mistaken, barely controlled. 'Alice assures me you're okay. Are you?'

'The baby's fine.' The all-important Karedes heir.

'Reassuring, but it wasn't my question.'

Oh, my, time for a deep breath. 'I have two bruised ribs.'

A few seconds' silence followed the revelation. 'Perhaps you'd care to give me your version of what happened.'

She did, in brief, and heard his husky oath in response.

'Obviously you chose not to drive.'

'Two flat tyres sort of precluded that.'

There was an electric silence. 'Would you care to run that by me again?'

'I've had it taken care of.'

'Why do I get the feeling there's a lot you're not telling me?'

And then some, Mia reiterated silently and rolled her eyes in exasperation.

'I assume you've reported both events to the police?'

'Not as yet.'

'I'll have Cris instigate enquiries, and I'll take the next flight out.'

'You're kidding me?'

He wasn't. 'I'll call you tomorrow.'

She'd suddenly had enough. 'There's no need.' She cut the call before he had a chance to respond.

The phone rang ten minutes later, and she exchanged glances with Alice. 'If it's Nikolos, I don't want to talk to him again tonight.'

Within seconds Alice held out the receiver. 'It's Cris.'

'News travels fast,' Mia said without preamble, and heard his faint chuckle.

'How are you?' There was concern apparent, and she dismissed her irritation. This was Cris…not Nikolos.

'I'm fine. Really,' she added.

'I'm glad. Meantime, we need to file a police report. I'll come over in the morning and bring someone with me.'

She took a deep breath, winced, and let it out carefully. Breathing deeply was not a good idea. 'I leave for work at eight.'

'Maybe you should consider taking the day off.'

This had gone far enough. 'Nikolos is indulging in a severe case of overkill.'

'And don't mess with me?' Cris queried with musing humour.

'Got it in one. I'm going to hang up now and go to bed. Goodnight, and—' she waited a beat '—thanks for the call.'

'Do you think that's wise?' Alice prompted as Mia made them each a cup of tea.

'Which particular part?'

'Why not go for broke?'

'I'd rather not discuss anything involving the name Karedes,' she declared darkly, and glimpsed her sister's faint smile.

'Like that, huh?'

Matt poked his head into the room. 'Good-night.'

'Sleep tight,' Mia bade lightly, and failed to raise a smile.

'You really are okay, aren't you?'

'Absolutely.' She lifted a hand and placed it over her heart. 'Promise.'

His sigh of relief was heartfelt. 'That's all right, then.' He even managed a smile before disappearing from sight.

'Cute kid,' Mia complimented when she was sure he was out of earshot. 'You're doing a great job with him.'

'He'd hate to hear you call him *cute*.'

It was Mia's turn to grin. 'I know. He's adorable.'

Alice stifled a smile. 'That, too.'

They sipped their tea in silence, then Mia turned towards her sister. 'Are you mad I asked Craig to visit on Sunday?'

'Nervous would be a better description.'

'You'll be with family and friends. It's not as if you're alone on a date with him.'

Alice became pale. 'I don't think I want to go there.'

'Take it one day at a time,' Mia offered gently, and stood up. 'I'll go key a fact-list into my laptop, and give Cris a disk.'

'You're really sure about work tomorrow?'

'Do you need to ask?'

'No, I guess not,' Alice said with resignation.

'Thanks for the hospital thing, and staying with me.' A warm smile curved her generous mouth. 'You were great.'

CHAPTER EIGHT

MIA woke next morning after a restless night's sleep, dressed, ate breakfast, and, following a close inspection of the Mercedes four-wheel drive, she took Alice's advice and drove to work.

Once there, she sent Cris a courtesy text message confirming she was at the pharmacy, then she donned her uniform and got on with the day.

One that became increasingly busy as morning shifted to afternoon, broken only by the appearance of Cris and a plainclothes policeman intent on filing a report of yesterday's assault.

It was late when she took her afternoon tea break, and she emerged from the staff-room ten minutes later to find the pharmacy manager deep in conversation with a dark-suited man whose stance and rear profile were all too familiar.

Nikolos.

Almost as if he sensed her presence, he turned towards her, and she could only stand there, momentarily incapable of moving as he closed the distance between them.

His expression was unfathomable, his eyes so dark they were almost black, and his mouth was set in lines that would instil fear into any adversary.

'Mia.' He lifted a hand and brushed gentle knuckles over her cheek. 'Go get your bag. You've finished for the day.'

'I—'

'Just do it, hmm?'

She wanted to protest, and almost did, except instinct warned against it. Instead she moved a fraction, caught the pharmacist's nod of approval, then she retrieved her bag from the staff-room and accompanied Nikolos out of the shop.

'How come you're back so soon?'

He cast her an all-encompassing look. 'I was in LA when I spoke to you last night.'

Had she any idea what he'd gone through in the last twenty-two hours? Imagining, fearing the worst, unable to see her, touch her? Totally reliant on verbal reassurances he knew could mask the true reality?

He'd made a few phone calls, pulled a few strings, and taken the next Sydney-bound flight out of LAX, arriving early afternoon. He'd caught a cab to his apartment, showered, dressed, and driven to the pharmacy where, Cris had text-messaged him, she'd ignored his directive and chosen to work.

He reached for her, closing his hands over her shoulders, then he slid each palm and cupped her face.

'*Theos,*' he uttered huskily as he smoothed a thumb-pad across each cheek. 'When I think what could have happened to you.'

His head lowered and his lips brushed hers, gently and with such care his touch was as light as a butterfly's wing.

It brought a faint sheen of unshed tears to her eyes, and she blinked rapidly to disperse them.

'I'm fine,' she managed shakily, knowing the words were a travesty. Right now she felt as if her bones were in the process of serious meltdown.

Nikolos traced the curve of her lower lip, felt it tremble, and he groaned as he trailed a path to the sweet hollow at the edge of her neck, savoured it, then he buried his mouth against the sensitive cord, nipped gently, and felt her body shake.

He wanted desperately what he knew he shouldn't take...and he told himself it was enough just to hold her, kiss her. For now.

Except he knew it would never be enough. For as long as he lived, he'd want, *need* her. In his life, his heart...dammit, in his bed.

He shifted slightly, and covered her mouth with his in a gentle exploratory kiss that teased with the evocative promise of passion...leashed and in control.

For her sake. He'd called in a favour and had a medic friend request a faxed copy of Mia's hospital medical record. Cris' faxed copy of the police report had been waiting for him when he'd first walked into his apartment a few hours ago. Together they detailed an account that chilled him to the bone, and added to a growing suspicion he entertained.

If he was correct...

Only a fool would act before there was sufficient proof, and no one could accord him a fool, he determined grimly.

It shouldn't take long. Days...possibly a week. Then he'd deal with it.

Meantime, he'd ensured there would be someone watching over her. For her own safety. Dammit, for his peace of mind.

The sound of voices, a car-horn blast brought their surroundings into sharp focus, and Nikolos effected a musing grimace. 'Let's get out of here.'

'The four-wheel drive is in the rear parking lot,' Mia indicated, only to have Nikolos catch hold of her hand and thread his fingers through hers as he turned her in the opposite direction.

'You're coming with me.'

'Unless you're intent on taking a circuitous route,' she ventured minutes later as his car gathered speed. 'You're going the wrong way.'

'We're going home. My home,' Nikolos corrected, and absorbed her sudden silence.

'I don't even know where that is.'

He spared her a quick glance. 'Seaforth. I have an apartment there.'

'I see.'

'That's it?'

'What would you have me say?' Mia queried, aware her pulse had quickened its pace. Every nerve-end seemed to quiver, heightening her senses to an almost uncomfortable pitch.

Was it inevitable, this crazy, wild feeling he was able to generate within her? To be affected to this extent was a madness she couldn't afford.

Mia focused her attention on the passing scene beyond the windscreen, noting the escalation in home style and value as they drew close to Seaforth.

Nikolos' apartment building was perched high overlooking Middle Harbour with splendid views of Port Jackson, and Mia didn't offer so much as a word as the Mercedes swept down into an underground car park.

If she had an ounce of sense, she'd insist he retrace the journey and take her to Alice's home. Except it was a bit late for that.

Maybe she could stop the lift at the main lobby, alight, and call a cab?

'Don't even think about it,' Nikolos warned as he summoned the lift.

'I'm not sure this is a good idea.' Too late, a tiny imp taunted. Much too late.

The lift doors opened, they stepped inside, and he depressed the uppermost button. The penthouse.

Electronic speed ensured they reached the top floor within seconds, and Mia preceded him into a spacious lobby, from which they entered a large, beautifully furnished lounge that at first glance combined a pleasing mix of beige, camel and cream.

She caught splashes of colour in paintings adorning the walls, and a wide expanse of tinted glass offering a panoramic view.

Had he employed a professional interior decorator? Or chosen the furnishings and colour scheme himself?

'It's beautiful,' she complimented, turning to face him, and felt her eyes widen as he shrugged off his jacket.

She watched as he tossed it over a nearby chair, and she was prepared to swear she stopped breathing when he took her bag and placed it onto the long buffet.

'Come here,' he bade gently as he caught hold of her hand and led her towards a large, comfortable sofa.

In one fluid movement he sank onto it and carefully pulled her onto his lap.

'Comfortable?'

There was something evocative about his warm strength, the feel of hard muscle and sinew caging her loosely within his grasp.

Mia breathed in the clean smell of him…freshly laundered cotton mingling with soap and the muskiness of his expensive cologne.

The temptation to curl into him and just *be* was almost too much to resist, and she held her breath as he tucked a fall of her hair back behind one ear.

She felt *safe*, in a way she never had before. As if nothing and no one could touch her while she was with him.

His lips brushed the top of her head, and he ran the palm of one hand down her thigh, lingered at her ankle, then eased one shoe off, then the other.

A sound that was part surprise, part resistance, passed her lips when he took her foot in one hand and used his thumb to massage the sole, gently working a kind of subtle magic over every bone in one foot before moving to render a similar treatment to the other.

Dear heaven, she could get used to this.

'Okay?'

Very much so. 'Are you trying to seduce me?'

'Is it working?'

She could almost hear the smile in his voice. 'I don't think I should answer that.'

'Care to fill me in on the past few days?'

She discovered a fascination for the fine stitching on the pocket of his shirt, and she traced the signature initial. 'Not particularly.'

Mia lifted her head and met his dark gaze. There were fine lines fanning out from the corner of his eyes, and the vertical groove on each cheek seemed deeper than she remembered. 'When did you last sleep?'

'Concern for my welfare, Mia?'

She ignored the query. 'Are you hungry?'

The edges of his mouth lifted. 'Now there's a question.'

'I'm talking *food*.'

'You want to go eat?'

'Depending what you have in your fridge and pantry, I could fix something.'

One eyebrow slanted as his eyes assumed a musing gleam. 'You really want to do this?'

If she remained held in his arms for much longer, it might not be a good thing. Already her resistance was in tatters, and staying with him wasn't an option. 'Yes.'

She wasn't prepared for the way his mouth closed over hers, or the slow, exploratory sweep of his tongue as he took evocative liberty with the moist cavern of her mouth in a kiss that made her ache for more.

Mia sensed rather than heard his faint groan, then he stood and placed her carefully on her feet. Bare feet, which diminished her height and made her incredibly aware of his height and breadth of shoulder.

'I guess it's the kitchen, huh?'

'Unless you want to change my mind?'

'I think something domestic is a wise choice,' she offered gravely.

Nikolos traced the edge of her jaw, lingered at the corner of her mouth, then let his hand drop. 'Wisdom, hmm?'

'I'll text message Alice and let her know I won't be home for dinner.'

The kitchen was a dream, with expensive appliances, a well-stocked fridge and pantry, and Mia set to work creating a meal from scratch. Pasta with a delicious sauce, garlic bread, and a steak salad to follow.

It was kind of nice to share the meal and clear up together afterwards. He made conversation easy...so easy she was scarcely aware of the passage of time until she happened to glance at her watch.

'I'll ring for a cab.'

'No, you won't.' He caught up his keys while she collected her bag.

Darkness had fallen, the sky a deep indigo with a sprinkling of stars. The view of the city night-scape was magical, and she paused to admire it as they walked through the lounge.

The basement car park was brightly lit, and their footsteps echoed in the concrete cavern. Minutes later Nikolos cleared security and took the Mercedes to street level.

It didn't take long to traverse the distance between Seaforth and Manly, and he parked close to the four-wheel drive.

'I'll collect you at six-thirty tomorrow evening.' He leaned in close and took her mouth in a brief, hard kiss. 'The pre-Christmas party, remember?'

He waited until she slid behind the wheel and ignited the engine, then he followed her to Alice's home and didn't drive off until she was safely indoors.

The evening had to be accorded an incredible success, Mia determined as she stood beside Nikolos in the large entertainment lounge of a beautiful home in suburban Woollahra.

It was clearly evident no expense had been spared with interior furbishing, with marble-tiled floors, magnificent marble pillars, exquisite French antique furniture, and works of art adorning the walls.

Fellow guests sipped champagne from crystal flutes and nibbled bite-size canapés as they touched base with friends and mingled.

The women were beautifully gowned, wonderfully bejewelled, and hair styled by whoever happened to be currently in vogue.

Skilfully applied make-up was an art form, and there were instances where Mia would have loved to take a woman aside, advise against a chosen toning and make suggestions to her benefit. A different, more subtle shade, a softer rouge application, and the eyes…the right touch and colour could work magic.

One matron came close to assuming clown-like features, for the colours and emphasis were a cosmetic disaster. While another had used such a heavy hand with the kohl and mascara wand, it was a travesty.

Use the magic, she wanted to offer, don't abuse it.

Was this how it was for each creator in a specific field? Did a seamstress cast a critical eye over the gowns, unconsciously noting flaws and making mental adjustments for improvement? Would a jewellery designer check cut, setting, and gem quality?

Going a step further, would a cosmetic surgeon subconsciously check for work done? An eyebrow lift, nose job, cheek implant?

'Having fun?'

Mia lifted her head a little, met Nikolos' musing gaze, and offered a warm smile. 'How could you imagine otherwise?'

His soft laugh stirred her senses and sent warmth singing through her veins. He had the craziest effect on her, everything about him as familiar to her as if they'd known each other in another lifetime.

Was that possible? Could it be she was fighting the inevitable?

Nikolos caught hold of her hand and lifted it to his lips. 'Don't ever change, *pedhi mou*.'

'A compliment?' She pressed a hand to her heart. 'I'm suitably charmed.'

His teeth nipped gently at her knuckles, then he soothed the faint mark with his tongue. 'Will you be quite so brave when I take you home?' He buried his lips in the palm of her hand. 'Mine,' he added as he lifted his head.

Mia felt her eyes widen as sensation arrowed through her body, activating all her fine nerve-ends until she became a quivering mess.

For several long seconds she was incapable of uttering a word, for there was instant vivid recall of the night they'd spent together, of how it had been between them...and the promise of how it would be again.

'Will you deny me? Yourself?'

Oh, dear God. 'You're giving me a choice?' Her voice was so quiet, it was little more than a whisper.

'You have doubts?'

She closed her eyes, then opened them again. The temptation to be with him, enjoy once again the intimacy they'd shared... dammit, she was pregnant with his child, for heaven's sake!

Could he even begin to comprehend just how much she wanted to be with him?

'Yes,' she said with simple honesty, 'because it would never be just one night.'

'And that would be so bad?'

She didn't answer. Couldn't.

'Nikolos.'

The feminine purr was all too familiar, and Mia felt her heart sink as she turned to find Anouska standing within touching distance.

The fashionista had outdone herself this evening in figure-hugging black. A strapless satin bustier showed her impressive breasts to maximum advantage while displaying a tiny waist, and a long black skirt was split almost to the hip-bone. Stiletto heels added to her majestic height, and her make-up was flawless.

'Darling, wonderful to see you. How was New York?'

Nikolos retained Mia's hand as he lowered his own. 'Anouska.'

Mia offered the polite smile, and barely refrained from gritting her teeth when Anouska traced the seam of Nikolos' jacket with the tip of a scarlet-lacquered nail.

'You haven't called me.'

Nikolos removed Anouska's hand.

The pout was pure Hollywood, and her eyes perfected a sultry pose. Practice makes perfect? Mia queried silently.

'I adore this time of year. So many functions. You *are* attending the awards presentation dinner next week?' She cast Mia a critical glance. 'You must find it difficult to find clothes, being so petite. I doubt even I could find anything suitable for you in my boutique.'

Cat's claws drawn and ready, Mia perceived, and faced the challenge with admirable panache.

'I mostly shop in the teen section, and leave my evening wear to a dressmaker.'

One eyebrow lifted with distinct disdain. 'You sew?'

'No,' she responded carefully. 'I have a friend who does.'

'Really?'

A friend who happened to be a well-known designer, whose clothes were sold in exclusive boutiques such as the one owned by Anouska.

In fact, unless she was mistaken, the gown Anouska wore was one of Lisa's designs.

A silent bubble of laughter rose in her throat at the irony of the situation.

Mia's gown bore classic lines in floral silk georgette with a fitted bodice and spaghetti straps, and a skirt whose hemline swirled with every move she made. The colours complemented the creamy texture of her skin, and she wore her hair in a simple knot atop her head, with diamond drop earrings and a diamond pendant that had belonged to her mother.

'The Parkinson-Stiles are throwing a tennis party on Wednesday evening. You'll be there, of course?'

'I'm afraid not.' Nikolos placed an arm around Mia's waist. 'If you'll excuse us?'

If looks could kill, Mia would have been struck dead on the spot. A shivery sensation slithered across the surface of her skin as she digested the venom evident momentarily before it was masked beneath a brilliant smile.

'Of course. Enjoy yourselves. I'll catch up with you later.'

Not if Mia could help it!

However, Anouska wasn't one to let opportunity slip through her fingers, and the fashionista managed to intrude more than once on one pretext or another.

'You're looking a little tired, poor darling. Is the social scene proving too much for you?'

Anouska's voiced concern was so artificial, Mia found it difficult to remain silent.

'I'm sure our hostess will accommodate you in one of her guest suites if you need to rest for an hour or two?'

'How considerate,' Mia managed sweetly, wondering if the other woman realised just how much of a challenge it was for her to be polite.

Nikolos brushed light fingers down her cheek and gave her a smile to die for. 'Home, hmm?' Nikolos declared gently. 'We'll locate our hosts and bid them goodnight.'

It took a while, and Mia waited until Nikolos eased the car out onto the street before venturing, 'Anouska has the hots for you.' And who could blame her?

'We're social acquaintances. Nothing more.'

Mia felt her stomach twist a little. 'She doesn't think so.'

'I've never given her any reason to believe otherwise.'

Perhaps not, she allowed dubiously. Yet it was obvious Anouska believed there was more to it than mere acquaintanceship. Much more. So much so, her overactive imagination had created something that didn't exist.

Mia tossed up whether she should relay Anouska's mid-week confrontation in the park, only to dismiss it. She'd dealt with the situation, and, besides, she could take care of herself. Hadn't she been doing so for years?

Yet there was a persistent niggle of disquiet, one she attempted to ignore as a sudden shower of rain splattered the windscreen, rendering the asphalt slick beneath the city street-lighting.

Nikolos traversed the Spit Bridge, then took the left fork to Seaforth and drove to his apartment building.

Mia cast him a studied look as he took the vehicle down into the underground car park. 'You don't play fair.'

He pulled into his allotted space and cut the engine. 'By making a decision?'

'One you've taken for granted is mutual.'

His eyes speared hers. 'You want to tell me it's not?'

She swallowed the sudden lump that had risen in her throat. *What are you waiting for?* an imp taunted. *You went with your instincts three months ago...why not now?*

Besides, her body was alive with a hunger only he could assuage. Need consumed her...need for his touch, his heat. *Him.*

'No.' She reached for the door-clasp and slid out from the passenger seat, then she walked at his side to the lift and rode with him to the uppermost floor.

Mia preceded him into the apartment, aware of subdued lighting, the almost silent electronic swish of drapes closing.

Now that she was here, the nerves in her stomach began an erratic dance, and she turned towards him, tentatively hesitant as he closed the distance between them.

Without a word he cupped her face and lay his mouth over hers, gently at first, savouring the taste and feel of her, without any pretence at haste.

Dear heaven, this was good. It was like coming home. Here was where she belonged, Mia decided hazily as she opened her mouth to him, glorying in the sensations he was able to evoke.

She closed her eyes and gave herself up to him, returning each kiss with a fervour that built the heat between them until there was need for more, much more than oral contact.

Clothes, she decided dimly. He was wearing too many clothes. With urgent fingers she pushed aside his jacket, and murmured her appreciation when he shucked it off and tossed it onto a nearby sofa.

His tie followed, and she busied herself releasing his shirt buttons, sighing a little when she slid the edges apart and she found warm satiny skin and hard muscle.

Mia pressed her mouth to one male nipple, suckled, then nipped with the edge of her teeth…and heard his husky groan.

Her hands went to his belt and slid the clip free, then she moved to his trousers and eased the zip fastening down over his straining arousal, exulting in the size and strength of it.

His trousers slipped to the carpet, and she traced the slender black silk band at his waist, the hem of his briefs, before feathering a light pattern over the thickened penis, feeling it engorge even further beneath her touch.

'This is a little one-sided, don't you think?' Nikolos murmured huskily as he settled his mouth in the delicate curve of her neck, ravished the throbbing pulse there, and felt her body buck in spontaneous reaction.

With swift movements he toed off his shoes, socks and stepped out of his trousers. His shirt landed on top of his jacket.

Gentle hands moved to the zip fastening of her gown and slid it free with practised ease, then he slipped the spaghetti straps over each shoulder and let the silky fabric slither down to the carpet.

All she wore beneath the gown was a silk and lace thong, and Nikolos traced its line to her waist and followed the lacy edge to her groin.

His touch was electric, and she shuddered as his fingers slid beneath the silk to touch her and explore the sensitive clitoris. A touch as light as a butterfly's wing, back and forth, in tight circles, until she went up and over in a series of orgasmic spasms that shook her very being, so that she held onto him in fear of falling.

With one fluid movement he swung her into his arms and carried her through to the master suite, holding her as he switched on the lights and crossed to the bed where he tossed back the bedcovers before lowering her gently down onto the silken sheets.

With careful fingers he traced the bruising on her ribcage, and uttered something indistinguishable beneath his breath.

Mia lifted a hand and touched a finger over his lips, and her eyes widened as the muscle bunched at the edge of his jaw.

Without a word he lowered his head and pressed fleeting kisses over the multicoloured mass, then he buried his head between her breasts before trailing a path to one peak.

The tightened bud engorged at his touch, and she cried out as he suckled, only to gasp when his fingers trailed low, stroking, caressing with increasing pressure until she went crazy with need, and began to plead with him. It was then he brushed his mouth down to the sensitive V and gifted her the most intimate kiss of all, savouring as he delighted in her pleasure.

Mia reached for him, and slowly, with infinite care, he entered her, restraining the need to surge in to the hilt.

Silken tissues stretched and expanded to accommodate him, and she dug her nails in deep as she urged him to a quicker pace.

He buried his mouth in the curve of her neck, nipped gently, and felt her response as he began to move, gently at first, then with controlled thrusts that took her to the heights of ecstasy and beyond.

It was a while before Nikolos disengaged from her, and she lifted a languid hand as she threaded fingers through his hair.

'Thank you.'

'For pleasuring you?'

Did she have any idea how beautiful she was? Or how wonderful she looked lying on his bed? He wanted to gather her up and keep her close for the rest of his life.

He lowered his head and brushed his lips to her breast, lingered there, then moved up to tease her mouth.

'That was all about me,' Mia said quietly, and she felt rather than saw his smile.

'We have the night, *agape*.'

'Uh-huh,' she murmured. 'Now I get to pleasure you.'

With one swift movement she rose and sat astride him, loving the way his eyes dilated and went dark as sin.

She adored the taste of him, the satiny texture of his skin, the flex of muscle and sinew as she explored every inch of him, taking her time and enjoying each hitch of his breath, and the faint groan that growled from his throat.

All the while he stroked her back, tracing the bones that made up her spine, circling the small indentations and gliding over smooth skin before tangling in her hair as he pulled her mouth down to his.

Did it get any better than this? Mia queried silently a long time later. What they shared wasn't just sex. It was something more, much more. *Wasn't it?*

Together they slept, then turned to each other again and again through the night.

In the dark hours of early morning they shared a leisurely shower, where after-play became foreplay, and there was something intensely pagan about making love beneath the beating flow of water.

Deliciously fun with the soft scent of soap, the lingering touch of skilful fingers, a long kiss that became something intensely intimate.

Afterwards, towelled dry, Mia fastened a towel, sarong-fashion, round her slender curves and began collecting her clothes.

'What do you think you're doing?'

She turned at the sound of Nikolos' husky voice, and gently shook her head. 'Dressing and going home.' Her mouth curved into a warm smile. 'I'll ring for a cab.'

He crossed to where she stood and curved his hands over her shoulders. 'Stay,' he said simply.

'I can't. Alice—'

'Will know you're with me.' His lips brushed hers, teased a little, then went in deep.

He bewitched her, totally, and she clung to him, uncaring when he loosened the towel and carried her back to bed.

Dawn fingered the earth with soft opalescent light, changing grey to colour, bringing the world alive for another day, and Mia stirred, felt Nikolos' arms tighten, and buried her head into the curve of his shoulder.

Soon she'd slip from the bed and text-message Alice, then she'd shower, dress and make breakfast.

Except she slept, and woke to find the bed empty, the teasing aroma of fresh coffee...and was that bacon?

She stretched, and felt the pull of muscles, the acute sensation deep within, and she closed her eyes against the vivid recollection of their lovemaking.

Lovemaking, she reiterated silently. Not just sex, or the shared indulgence of intimacy.

Where did they go from here?

Oh, hell. What was the time? She twisted her head and checked the digital clock, groaned out loud, then she slipped out of bed, hit the shower, then, dry, she wound a towel round her slender form and made her way out to the kitchen.

Nikolos was dressed in chinos and a polo shirt, looking disgustingly healthy and re-laxed, given the amount of sleep he'd had.

He turned as she entered the room. 'Hi.' He crossed to her side and covered her mouth with his own.

Hmm, she could get used to this!

'Bacon and eggs, toast, tea.' He swept an arm to the table set for two.

And coffee. What she wouldn't give for a brimming cup of strong black sweet coffee. Instead she slid into a chair and settled for tea.

'I rang Alice.'

Mia wondered at her sister's reaction, and decided Alice would approve. 'She's plan-ning a barbecue. I really need to be there soon to help out.' The tea was great. Not as great as coffee, but it would do. She picked up cutlery and began doing justice to the con-tents on her plate.

'We'll leave after we've eaten.' He waited a beat. 'It'll give you time to pack.'

Pack? 'Nikolos—'

'I want you in my life, Mia,' he said gently. 'I need to be in yours.' He held her gaze. 'For all the right reasons.'

Move in with him? The thought of making the apartment her home, returning here after work each night, *sleeping* with him… Should she take that step? *Dared* she?

'After last night, you want us to live apart?'

Occupy a lonely bed, wishing she were with him? Living in denial? Why? As a matter of principle?

Innate honesty came to the fore. 'No.'

His smile almost undid her. 'Marry me.'

Mia's lips parted, and her eyes widened into deep dark pools.

He trailed light fingers down her cheek. 'The ball is in your court, *agape mou.*'

She wasn't capable of saying a word. Instead, she caught hold of his hand and pressed her lips to his palm.

CHAPTER NINE

MATT raced out front as soon as Nikolos pulled into the kerb. 'Hi.'

Mia slid out from the passenger seat and gave her nephew a hug. 'When are your friends due?'

'In about an hour. Mum bought me a new game for my PlayStation.' He smiled as Nikolos crossed to Mia's side. 'It's great to see you.'

'Likewise. Which games do you have?'

Male bonding between man and boy, Mia mused, hoping Craig Mitchell would be as successful at it. 'I'll leave you two to chat while I go help Alice.'

Mia went into the house and made her way through to the kitchen where her sister was putting the finishing touches to a superb-looking dessert.

'I'm sorry I wasn't here to help,' Mia said quietly.

Alice shot her a genuinely surprised look. 'Why? Getting it together with Nikolos is the best thing that could happen to you.'

'You think so?'

'Mia—*yes*. How could you doubt it?'

'You can't agree this is a normal relationship,' she ventured, watching as her sister checked a list.

'You had normal,' Alice reminded. 'We both did. Neither worked out.'

'He's asked me to move in with him.'

Alice didn't miss a beat. 'I hope you said yes.'

A tiny smile lifted the edges of her mouth. 'Trying to get rid of me, huh?'

'Wanting the best for you,' Alice assured gently.

Mia looked at the salads, the bread rolls ready to pop into the oven when needed. 'What can I do?'

'It's all done. Except the outdoor table. You can put out plates and flatware, and the unbreakable glasses.' She indicated a high cupboard. 'They're up there. And the paper napkins,' she added.

It was only a small get-together, with four of Matt's friends and their parents, Matt's tennis coach and his fiancée, and Craig Mitchell.

A pleasant number to mix and mingle and get acquainted, Mia acknowledged, admiring the apparent ease with which Alice organised the food and ensured everyone had plenty to drink, as well as overseeing the boys.

Her sister was an excellent home-maker, and a born mother who should have a brood of children to love, supervise and care for.

Why did some of the good people make bad choices in life?

Nikolos and Craig hit it off very well, and Mia was taken by the lawyer's casual attempt to empathise with Matt. He had just the right approach, and didn't try too hard…there, interested, but not intrusive.

'Playing matchmaker?' Nikolos queried quietly as they carried bowls of leftover salad into the kitchen.

Concern clouded her features. 'Is it obvious?'

He removed the bowls from her hands and drew her in close. 'No.' He dropped a kiss on the tip of her nose. 'He seems a nice guy.'

'I'd love to see Alice happy.' The temptation to lean into him was difficult to resist. 'We'd better get back out there.'

Nikolos let her go, and followed her outdoors. The boys were kicking a soccer ball around the yard, and Nikolos joined Craig and the tennis coach in passing the ball.

'They're having a good time,' Alice commented, and Mia squeezed her sister's shoulder.

'It's great. Fantastic food, as always, and plenty of it.' She paused, then added quietly, 'Craig is enjoying himself.'

'He seems to be.'

'If he asks you out, I'll come sit with Matt.'

'I don't think—'

'Promise me you won't say no.'

'Maybe,' Alice compromised, and frowned slightly at Mia's light laugh. 'What's so funny?'

'We're giving each other advice on relationships.'

It was after four when everyone began to leave, and five when Craig drove away.

'Wasn't that cool?' Matt asked as they went indoors.

'Really cool,' Mia agreed.

'There's steak and marinated chicken in the fridge we didn't need to use.' Alice tied on an apron and began stacking the dishwasher. 'Why don't you both stay for dinner? Unless you have plans?'

'No plans,' Nikolos assured.

'Want to come see my new PlayStation game?' Matt suggested with boyish eagerness, and Nikolos offered an easy grin.

'Thought you were never going to ask.'

Together Mia and Alice cleaned up, working with familiar co-ordinated ease until the kitchen and outdoor area resembled its usual ordered appearance.

Laughter and hoots of victory echoed from Matt's room, and Alice rolled her eyes expressively.

They ate at a reasonable hour, given Matt was due in school the next day.

Nikolos appeared relaxed and totally at ease, and Mia was supremely conscious of him, the warmth of his smile, the gleaming amusement in his dark gaze whenever their eyes met.

Was his mind straying towards what they'd shared through the night...and would inevitably share again a few hours from now?

Even the mere thought caused sensual heat to radiate through her body, and whenever her gaze slid to his mouth she had instant recall of the wicked pleasures he could bestow.

One look was all it took, and she became incandescent with primitive desire, so intense she had to wonder if it was recognisable...and inwardly died a hundred deaths at the possibility.

Matt went off to bed at eight, and not long afterwards Mia collected some of her clothes, make-up and toiletries, and left a few things residing in the wardrobe and dressing-table.

Then it wasn't a complete move, she told herself as she filled two large holdalls. Leaving stuff behind meant she still had a place to go to, a bolt-hole should she need it.

Yet the act of moving in with Nikolos made a statement. Just take things day by day, Mia bade silently. Living with him wasn't the final commitment of marriage. She would be free to leave, just as he would be free to tell her to go.

And that was a sobering thought. What if she didn't want to leave? Ever?

Oh, for heaven's sake! Now she was attempting to reach into the future and predict the unpredictable.

'Need some help?'

Mia turned at the sound of Alice's voice and offered a bright smile. 'All done. I've left a few things.'

'It'll always be your room,' Alice reminded quietly, and Mia gave her a hug.

'You're the best.'

'Ditto.'

'I'll ring tomorrow evening.' Mia's smile was wickedly mischievous. 'You can update me on Craig.'

'Oh, sure. Like all of a sudden he's going to change from boss to new best friend?'

'Don't underestimate him.'

They emerged from the bedroom, each with a holdall in one hand, which Nikolos captured as they entered the lounge.

It had been a lovely day, and Mia said so as Alice accompanied them to the front door.

Minutes later Nikolos slung the holdalls into the back of his car, and indicated the four-wheel drive. 'I'll follow you.'

It didn't take long to reach Seaforth, and he swung in front of her when they reached his apartment building, allowing her to follow him down into the basement car park and park immediately adjacent his allotted space.

This was it, Mia contemplated silently as they rode the lift. One step forward to the temporary commitment. The Karedes matriarchs would be pleased.

Had Nikolos apprised them of the move?

'Not yet,' Nikolos drawled as they exited the lift and entered his apartment.

'A man of many talents,' Mia accorded lightly. 'You read minds.'

'Yours has a certain transparency.' He closed the door and placed both holdalls onto the floor. 'Come here.'

He moved in close and lowered his head to hers, taking possession of her mouth in a kiss that took hold of any doubts and dismissed them.

Mia felt as if she were drowning in a pool of emotional sensation, and she clung to him, wanting more, so much more.

She needed to feel his skin without the restriction of clothing, to kiss and caress each pulse-point, until he lost control. She wanted his mouth on her, driving her wild as they both went up in flames.

There was only Nikolos, the moment, and a wealth of sensual pleasure as he swept her into his arms and carried her down to the bedroom.

Living with Nikolos was so much more than Mia had expected. There was no doubt good sex…*lovemaking*, she amended with a secret smile, acted as a powerful aphrodisiac.

To be woken early each morning with a lover's touch made for a wonderful start to the day. Days when serving difficult customers and soothing fractious ones didn't faze her at all.

As to the nights…Mia fixed dinner if they stayed in, and when they dined out they chose a small intimate restaurant away from the glitzy social scene. Evenings that became an anticipatory tease to the lovemaking they would share on arriving home.

Socialising as such didn't exist during that initial week, although their absence from the social scene couldn't last overlong.

The Karedes empire supported a few well-known charities, there were certain social obligations, especially with Christmas only a matter of weeks away. Then there were family.

News of Nikolos' and Mia's cohabitation had reached the Karedes matriarchs, which resulted in pressure to confirm a suitable evening to visit.

Craig Mitchell's invitation to have Alice join him for dinner proved a highlight.

'Told you so.' Mia's soft laugh held delight Monday evening. 'When, where? What are you going to wear? Do you want me to come sit Matt, or—?' Inspiration struck. 'He could have a sleep-over, and I'll drive him home next day.'

'Whoa,' Alice cautioned. 'One, it's a week night, which means school the next morning. And two, I haven't said I'll go.'

'Alice!' The reprimand held a note of despair. *'Go.'* She was only just getting started. 'Nikolos won't mind, and I'll drop him to school on my way to work.'

'But what—'

'No *but*,' Mia insisted. 'I'll personally come over there and *shake* you if you refuse.'

Nikolos wandered into the room and stood regarding her with amusement. She was a pocket dynamo. Earthy, loyal, honest, loving... Sexy, sensual. *His.*

He could imagine her going toe-to-toe with anyone who dared question the integrity of anyone she loved. As a mother, she'd beat a lioness hands down.

Attired in jeans, a cotton knit top, her hair tied back in a pony-tail, face free of make-up, she looked about sixteen.

She was an easy read, with expressive features, a generous mouth and eyes a man could drown in. He adored the sound of her voice, her laugh, the way she tilted her chin when she was about to argue. And he loved the way she loved.

To reach out in the night and know she was there, to curl her in close against him and rest his cheek on her head. To hold her, and delight in her response.

'What was that all about?' Nikolos drawled as he crossed to her side when she cut the call.

'Craig has asked Alice out.'

He curved an arm round her shoulders and pulled her in. 'Why should that upset you?'

'She has cold feet.'

'Which you intend to rectify by...doing what?'

His hands were effecting a soothing magic across her back, and she felt her bones begin to melt. 'You're trying to distract me.'

'Is it working?'

Oh, yes. It would be all too easy to lean in against him, link her hands at his nape and pull his head down to hers. 'Is it okay if Matt has a sleep-over here?'

Nikolos hid a smile at her resistance, knowing what it cost her. 'Of course. When?'

'This week. If I can persuade Alice to accept.'

He nuzzled his lips against the curve of her neck, and felt her go limp. Better. 'And if she doesn't?'

'I'll work on her.' She groaned as his hands slipped beneath her top and sought the clip fastening on her bra.

'I don't suppose you're interested in coffee?'

'My sole interest right now is *you*.' His fingers freed the top button of her jeans.

'You're insatiable.' The breath hitched in her throat as he lay a hand against her stomach.

His mouth touched hers fleetingly, hovered, then settled for a few minutes. 'You want me to stop?'

'Don't even think about it.'

He swung her into his arms and made his way towards the bedroom. 'That's what I thought.'

Mia's hands were as quick and deft as his own in discarding clothes, and she followed him down onto the bed, pinned his arms above his head with one hand, then freed the band from her hair with the other.

She watched his eyes darken as she slowly lowered her head and brushed her hair back and forth across his chest, teasing its length against his male nipples before releasing his hands and sweeping her hair lower, down his ribcage to his waist, the thick length of his engorged penis, to the nest of male hair couching his scrotum.

Seconds later she dipped her head low and used her mouth in an inventive evocative tasting that tested his control and broke it.

Her pleasure was short-lived as he rolled her onto her side and entered her in one slow thrust, only to ease back as he initiated a teasing foreplay that drove her wild.

It was a while before he took her over the edge, joined her there, and held her as she fell.

Afterwards as she lay supine he brushed his lips over every inch of her, slowly and with infinite care, before settling just above her navel.

Mia felt his lips move and sensed rather than heard the sound of his voice. She lifted a languid hand and threaded her fingers through his hair, lightly exploring the slight hollows in his head.

'Did you say something?'

He trailed a path of soft kisses to her waist-line, then lifted his head to look at her. 'Just assuring our son or daughter of a loving welcome into the world.' And how he intended to take good care of their child's mother.

It undid her, and she was powerless to prevent the faint shimmering tears, or the single one spilling to run across her temple.

Nikolos saw it, and he swore softly as he gathered her in and pulled up the covers. She surprised and amazed him with her strength and her fragility. A single tear, and he was affected more than by anything she could have said.

She slept, so still and quiet, her body curled into his, and when she stirred in the early morning hours he carried her through to the *en suite* and shared her shower.

Breakfast was a leisurely meal eaten out on the terrace overlooking the inner harbour. The sun shone, its warmth holding the promise of a wonderful summer's day.

'I need to confirm dinner with Sofia,' Nikolos indicated as he drained his coffee. 'Towards the end of the week okay with you?'

She could do this. 'I guess so.' Sofia wasn't nearly as fearsome as Angelena, in whose eyes Mia must surely have taken a step in the right direction from 'one night stand' to 'live-in lover'. Without doubt there would be hope for the transition to 'wife'.

Nikolos stood up, caught up his jacket and shrugged it on, then he crossed to her side and bestowed a brief hard kiss. 'Have a good day, hmm?'

'You, too.'

It didn't take long to clear the table and load the dishwasher, then she put the finishing touches to her make-up, caught up her shoulder-bag, and took the lift down to the car park.

Mia checked her cellphone for text messages during her lunch break. There were two…the first from Nikolos indicating he'd be caught up in a late-afternoon meeting and wouldn't be home until seven. The second came from Alice, requesting Matt sleep over Wednesday evening.

She'd done it! Knowing Alice as she did, it had taken considerable courage to accept Craig's invitation. She just hoped Alice's boss had the patience to take things slow.

The day had suddenly become brighter, and Mia spent the afternoon in the dispensary assisting with prescriptions at a preliminary level. It was interesting work, matching various drugs to the doctor's diagnosis and checking contra-indications, discussing with the pharmacist how the drug would work, examining the correct dosage, the patient's medication history logged into the computer. What over-the-counter medications conflicted with prescribed medication.

It was a constant learning curve, a challenge that held her intense interest.

Her dream was to own a pharmacy and design the shop fittings to maximum advantage. For the pharmacist, the assistants, the customers.

Security cameras, video surveillance, panic buttons were par for the course with crime and theft at a high level in today's society.

Mia was beginning to recognise the regular customers, mostly residents living close by. There were the usual drive-bys, people who needed aspirin or plasters, cough medicine.

It was close to five when a familiar figure entered the shop, and Mia's heart sank as she recognised Anouska.

This couldn't be good. What could the fashionista possibly want in this particular shop, if not to cause mischief and mayhem? It was merely a matter of what and when.

At first Anouska appeared to be examining products in the personal hygiene section, then she moved to a stand stacked with packets of prophylactics, selected a variety, then crossed to the counter.

One of the assistants had left early, and the one remaining was busy serving a customer. Which left Mia to step down from the dispensary and tend to Anouska's purchase.

Smile politely, pop the packets in the appropriately sized bag, take the money, and extend the usual pleasantries.

Three, four minutes, and Anouska would be out the door.

Except that wasn't part of Anouska's plan.

'You can guarantee these, I assume?'

Here we go, Mia concluded silently. 'The packet carries instructions for correct usage.'

'They are...resilient and good quality?'

'We only carry quality brands.'

Anouska's mouth thinned. 'Pity you didn't choose wisely when you purchased your own.' Her voice rose when Mia declined to comment. 'But then I imagine falling pregnant was your aim.'

'Your remarks are insulting and uncalled for,' Mia said quietly.

'Really? It's you who is insulting.' She beckoned the pharmacist in the dispensary. 'I want to lodge a complaint.'

To give the pharmacist his due, he listened carefully, explained Mia had not acted in an untoward manner, and suggested Anouska complete her purchases or reject them.

Without a word the fashionista turned and walked out of the shop.

Mission achieved...sort of.

'I'm sorry,' Mia offered, and met the pharmacist's raised eyebrows.

'Whatever for? You weren't at fault.'

Yes, she was. Merely for being in the way of Anouska's objective…Nikolos. What bothered her was the purpose behind the fashionista's visit.

She didn't have long to find out. Half an hour later when she crossed to the car park there was a police car lined up close to the four-wheel drive, with two uniformed officers in attendance. One was taking down details from a man dressed in jeans and tee shirt, while the other was standing guard over a loud-mouthed female vilifying both officers and the witness with deplorable language.

Recognition was immediate. *Anouska?*

At that moment the fashionista turned, saw her, and began screaming a stream of invective. Whereupon the officer cuffed her and pushed her into the rear of the police car.

Mia crossed to the four-wheel drive and was sickened by the words scoured in the metalwork.

'Mia Fredrickson? This woman was caught causing damage to the four-wheel drive registered in your name.' The officer indicated the man who'd just given his statement. 'Your bodyguard has provided us with details, photographic and video evidence.'

Bodyguard?

'Nikolos Karedes hired me.'

At that moment Nikolos' Mercedes pulled into an adjacent space, and Mia watched as he crossed to the group.

'Officers. Jake.'

He caught hold of Mia's hand and lifted it to his lips. 'Mia.'

'Miss Fredrickson has only recently arrived on the scene.'

'Perhaps,' she said in measured tones, 'you might care to explain why this man—' she indicated Jake '—is acting as a bodyguard. Specifically, *my* bodyguard.'

Nikolos' eyes darkened for an instant, then he moved his gaze to the police officers. 'There's no need for either of us to stay?'

'We'll require a statement from you, sir, regarding background facts. Tomorrow? Meantime, you're free to go.'

'Jake, you'll take care of the car?'

'Already organised.'

'Thanks.' Nikolos led her towards the Mercedes, saw her seated inside, then he took the wheel and vacated the car park.

'You'd better give me some answers.'

'I'm sure you're sufficiently astute to have arrived at a few of them,' he indicated as he headed towards Seaforth. 'There was suspicion Anouska damaged the tyres, and paid that young thug to attack you. I hired Jake to run surveillance for your protection.' He eased to a halt at a set of traffic lights. 'Anouska's vehicle was parked several metres down the street from Alice's home on more than one occasion. At night. Last Sunday. She has also been keeping watch on my apartment building at night and in the early hours of the morning.' The lights changed and the car sprang forward. 'This afternoon she visited the pharmacy, then she crossed to the car park and used a metal object to scour marks on the bodywork.'

'You needed to catch her in the act,' Mia said dully.

'Yes.'

'You could have told me.'

'It was considered best not to unduly alarm you.'

'Best by *whom*?' she demanded.

'Everyone involved.'

She shot him a sharp glance. 'Alice knew?'

'No. The police psychiatrist pinned you as the target.'

'Great.'

'You were never in danger at any time.'

He'd made sure of it, and she fell quiet for several minutes.

The sequence of recounted scenes sped through her mind, and she felt the sudden rise of nausea. 'I think I'm going to be sick.'

Please, God, please don't let it happen, not here, not *now*.

She undid her seat belt as Nikolos pulled into the kerb, and she made it out of the car…just.

Seconds later Nikolos was there, and she motioned him aside. Not that he took any notice, and when she was done she directed huskily, 'My bag. There's tissues, wet wipes. Bottled water.'

He fetched them, and minutes later she felt measurably better. 'Let's get out of here.'

As soon as she entered the apartment she made straight for the shower, brushed her teeth, used a mouthwash for good measure, then she stepped into comfortable jeans and a tee shirt.

At least her stomach appeared to have settled, which had to be a good thing, she decided as she emerged into the bedroom.

Nikolos was there, prowling, his expression faintly grim as she met his gaze. 'Maybe I should call the obstetrician.'

'Pregnant women throw up on occasion. It's called morning sickness. Except that tends to be a misnomer, as it's known to happen at any time of the day or night.' She took a calming breath. 'I'll go fix something for dinner.'

'Forget it. We'll order in.'

'Continue treating me like a fragile flower, and I'll hit you.'

'That could prove interesting.'

'Count on it.' With that Mia walked out to the kitchen ahead of him.

It didn't take long to grill a couple of steaks, assemble a salad, and heat bread rolls.

'I thought you were supposed to be at a meeting?'

'I walked out of it when Jake called.'

She handed him a plate. 'Go sit down.' She took her own plate and carried the salad bowl to the table.

Cable television provided visual entertainment for a while, and although Mia was prepared to swear she only closed her eyes for a few seconds she barely stirred as Nikolos took her to bed.

'Hey,' she protested as he began removing her clothes. 'I can do that.'

'Sure you can,' he said gently and continued divesting each garment. Then he slid her beneath the covers, undressed, and joined her.

He was wonderful, warm, and solid, and she nestled close, and slept.

CHAPTER TEN

MATT'S sleep-over proved a huge success. He loved the apartment, whistled at Nikolos' electronic equipment, ate well, and together they took it in turns to challenge each other's skills with chess. He didn't even protest when Mia called 'bedtime', and later when she checked on him he lay still and contented in sleep.

'No problems?' Nikolos queried when she sank onto the sofa at his side.

'None.'

He curved an arm around her shoulders and brushed his lips to her temple. 'He adores you.'

'It's mutual,' Mia responded simply as she leaned in against him. His warmth held a sensual potency that succeeded in quickening her pulse and heightened all her nerve-ends.

It was magical, witching, primitive and raw. A combination that excited and frightened, soothed and enticed.

The night she'd discovered Nikolos was Cris' brother had been one of the worst nights of her life. Now, she didn't want to imagine a night without him. An admission she chose not to examine too closely just yet. Although putting it off wouldn't achieve a thing.

'Sofia has invited us to join her for dinner tomorrow evening.'

Now there was something to think about! 'A verbal sparring session with the Karedes matriarchs, huh?' Her voice was light, almost teasing as her eyes met his, and she smiled at his musing chuckle.

'It'll be a breeze.'

Much to Mia's surprise, he was right. Cris' friendship was a given, and Sofia exuded friendly warmth over pre-dinner drinks. Even Angelena appeared suitably restrained during the excellent three course meal.

The 'marriage' subject didn't arise, nor was 'wedding' mentioned.

Nikolos had, without doubt, issued specific instructions, which even the irascible Angelena chose to observe.

It had been a pleasant evening, and Mia said so as Nikolos traversed the Harbour Bridge *en route* to the northern suburbs. The night was clear with a sprinkling of stars, the precursor to another fine summer's day.

The following two days involved split shifts to accommodate one of the pharmacy assistants, which meant working Friday morning and Saturday afternoon, and she'd made arrangements to catch up with Alice early on Saturday. Phone calls were fine, but they didn't compensate for meeting in person.

Which they did, sharing morning tea in the tennis clubhouse while Matt had his coaching lesson.

'Craig,' Mia began with a mischievous smile. 'The nitty-gritty,' she teased. 'Not the condensed version.'

'He's…nice,' Alice allowed. 'Kind. Thoughtful.'

'You're describing your boss. I want Craig, the man.'

'He was a gentleman.'

'Didn't kiss you, huh?'

She saw the faint tinge of pink colour her sister's cheeks.

'He's asked Matt and I to a picnic on Sunday.'

Way to go, Craig! This was looking good. 'Naturally you said yes.'

'It should be a pleasant day,' Alice admitted, and rolled her eyes expressively as Mia gave an outrageous grin. 'Your turn.'

'Okay.'

'That's it? *Okay?* How come I get to spill and you don't?'

There was never going to be a better opportunity. 'I guess I'm having a hard time coming to terms with a relationship that doesn't conform with the norm,' she said slowly.

'What's normal? We both had that first time round. The getting-to-know-you, the courtship, engagement. I did the marriage thing.' Alice leaned forward. 'Didn't work for either of us.'

'I imagined falling in love as a gradual thing, something that begins with friendship and develops over time.'

'Not meeting someone and *knowing* in the depths of your soul they're *the one*?'

'Can it be that simple?' Mia queried. A recognition of sexual chemistry...yes. But *love*?

'Sometimes I think it can,' Alice said gently.

'It seems too—' She paused, hesitating over the choice of words.

'Too much, too soon? Too easy?' Her sister leaned forward, her gaze intent. 'Could you live without Nikolos?'

She didn't have to think. 'No.'

'Would you want to?'

Anguish welled up inside and threatened to tear her apart.

'So,' Alice demanded gently. 'What are you waiting for?'

Nothing, absolutely nothing. 'I need to make a phone call.'

It took only seconds to key in the necessary digits, another few to connect.

'Karedes.'

'Is this a good time?' Oh, hell, don't weaken now. 'It's Mia.'

How could she believe he required identification, when the sound of her voice was as familiar to him as his own? Each cadence, the light in her laughter, the warmth when she uttered his name…and the mesmeric hunger when he held her in the throes of passion.

She had the power to turn his world upside down, then send it spinning out of control. It wasn't a feeling he was comfortable with, but one he'd no doubt become accustomed to…eventually, he determined. Maybe by the time he dangled their grandchild on his knee.

Humour at that thought curved his mouth into a musing smile. 'It depends what you have in mind.'

How could she say *I love you* over the phone? 'Would it cause a problem if we cancel tonight?'

Given the nature of the fund-raiser, he could easily send in a cheque. 'Do I get to ask why?'

'I'll explain later. Bye.'

The afternoon became a blur as she summoned Alice's assistance, made phone calls, and begged an hour's grace on her usual finishing time.

Alice, bless her, was waiting in the lobby when Mia arrived there, and together they rode the elevator to Nikolos' penthouse apartment.

'Go shower and change,' Alice instructed. 'I'll take care of the table, and transfer everything into serving dishes.'

Half an hour later Mia emerged into the kitchen wearing minimum make-up, lip-gloss and a touch of eyeshadow. She'd wound her hair into a knot atop her head, and slipped into black evening trousers and a silk camisole.

'Seriously *wow*,' Alice complimented. 'Okay, I'm out of here.'

'Thanks.' Mia's gratitude was heartfelt. 'I couldn't have done it without you.'

She had five minutes, maybe ten, before Nikolos would walk through the door. Time enough to pen the words she wanted to write on a card.

A quick glance at the table revealed Alice had thought of everything, right down to the candles, a delicate centrepiece, gleaming cutlery and crystal.

Nerves were a curse, and hers were waging a war second to none.

What if…? *Don't,* she cautioned silently. There are no *what ifs*.

The sound of a key sliding into the lock heralded Nikolos' arrival, and she summoned a winsome smile as he crossed to her side.

'Hmm,' he managed appreciatively as he reached for her. His lips brushed hers, settled, then went in deep, in an evocative exploration that made her almost forget her plans for the evening.

'I can't persuade you to share my shower?' His hands slid to her waist and held her there.

'Been there, done that,' Mia responded lightly, sinking in against him, loving the way his hands trailed a light pattern over her back. 'And you have ten minutes.' She pressed a kiss to the edge of his jaw. 'Go.'

Bread rolls into the oven, open the wine and let it breathe, check on the dessert...

Mia lit the candles, then transferred serving dishes onto the table as Nikolos entered the kitchen.

The tailored business suit had been replaced with chinos and a chambray shirt, and he'd shaved, his hair still damp from his shower.

Just one look at him, and her bones began to melt.

'Need some help?'

'All done.'

He moved in close and trailed light fingers down her cheek. 'You're nervous. Why?'

It would be so easy to link her hands at his nape and pull his head down to hers.

Except then they wouldn't eat, the food would spoil…and, besides, she wanted to follow the plan.

'I haven't done this before.' Honesty was easy.

Nikolos' mouth curved into a musing smile as he traced her lower lip. 'What, precisely?'

The familiar quickened beat of her heart was visible in the hollow beneath her throat, and she swallowed compulsively in an effort to control it.

Did he know? Could he guess? 'Bear with me,' she managed after a few timeless seconds, silently begging him to understand.

'Would you have me sip through a glass of wine while we indulge in a recap of each other's day?' he queried lightly as he moved to the table and poured a measure of clear amber liquid into one of the crystal goblets. 'Or shall we hold a discussion over the meal?'

There was bottled water reposing next to the wine, and Nikolos filled a glass and handed it to her, then touched its rim with his own.

'*Salute.*' His gaze speared hers, and narrowed slightly as he glimpsed the faint tinge of pink colouring her cheeks. 'A busy day?'

'Some,' she agreed. 'I enjoy working in a smaller suburban pharmacy. The customers are mostly local residents.' As conversation, it seemed incredibly banal, and she indicated the serving dishes.

'Let's eat.' Otherwise she'd never last the distance.

The food had to be wonderful, given Alice's flair for fine cuisine, but Mia barely tasted a thing as she sampled the starter and forked a few mouthfuls from the main course before pushing her plate to one side.

'I'll get dessert.'

'Dessert can wait,' Nikolos declared with deceptive mildness. 'Suppose you tell me why you've been treading eggshells for the past half-hour.'

Oh, hell. The moment of truth! With care she slid the envelope from beneath her side plate. 'I wanted to give you this.' She held it out to him, and watched as he leant forward to take it.

Mia searched his features, watching for the slightest change in expression, and glimpsed none as he slid open the flap and extracted the card.

Choosing it had been a mission, as she'd searched numerous racks, discarding humour for conventional, then changing her mind countless times before selecting a blank card featuring a Monet print.

The words she'd written were engraved in her mind.

I love you with all my heart. Will you marry me and share the rest of my life?

Each second seemed to take for ever as he opened the card, and her heart leapt to her throat.

At last he lifted his head, and his dark eyes met and held her own. 'Thank you.'

She was going to die if he didn't add something...*anything*.

'You doubt my answer?'

Mia made a helpless gesture, unable to trust her voice.

'You think I could make love to another woman the way I make love to *you*? *Theos*.' The husky epithet held a silken savagery as he rose to his feet. 'Or the child you carry is more important to me than its mother?'

His eyes blazed with unrestrained passion...and something else, much deeper and more profound. 'You're the other half of my soul. My heart.' He crossed to her side and drew her to her feet. 'My life.'

Mia was aware of warmth coursing through her veins, heating her body as it reached every nerve-end. Mesmeric, intensely sensual…passion at its zenith on every level. Of the mind, the heart.

'I love you,' Nikolos said gently. 'I always will. Believe it.'

His mouth took possession of hers with a hunger that was witching, shameless, and she became lost in the rapture of his touch.

His, for a lifetime.

'You sweet fool,' Nikolos chastised in a voice husky with emotion. 'How could you not have known how I feel about you?'

She wound her arms round his neck, lifted her body against his, wrapped her legs around his waist, and hung on as he made his way to the bedroom.

'Mmm.' This was good, better than *good*. It was like reaching for the stars and catching hold of the sun, the moon…the entire universe. She nuzzled his earlobe, nipped, then soothed it with her tongue. 'I wasn't sure you needed *me*.'

Seconds later he gently disentangled her arms, her legs, then slid her down to her feet.

'I'll show you.'

He did. Very thoroughly. And they never got to eat dessert.

It was in the early pre-dawn hours when Mia drifted into semi-wakefulness and became aware of her surroundings, the bed, and the muscular arm that enfolded her close, even in sleep, against a warm, strong, intensely male body.

Love, she determined wistfully, was a wondrous entity. Tenuous, and so infinitely precious. An emotion that should never be taken for granted.

Nikolos was her life, her reason for being. Friend, lover, soul-mate. Always.

Reflective thought drifted slowly through her mind as she recaptured the night they first met, and the force of her cataclysmic reaction.

It was almost as if destiny had played a part, putting them both in the same place at the same time, with fate lending a hand to ensure they met again.

A musing smile played across her generous mouth as she recalled her reluctance to have anything to do with Nikolos Karedes.

Yet he had persisted, dispensing with her resistance as if it was nothing of consequence.

When had she fallen in love with him? More importantly, when had she known it was *love*?

'What are you thinking, *agape mou*?'

The sound of his drawled voice held a musing indulgent quality as he switched on the bedside lamp.

'You heard me *thinking*?' she couldn't help teasing.

The soft light illuminated the room, and she watched as he rolled onto his side and brushed gentle fingers down her cheek. Her mouth quivered as he traced its outline and lingered at one edge.

'I was already awake.' He'd felt a change in the depth of her breathing, registered its quickened pace.

'I love you.' There, she'd said it. Three little words, yet they proved the hardest ones for her to vocalise.

His eyes darkened and became almost black with emotion.

'I tried so hard not to,' she managed with innate honesty.

He leant down and brushed his mouth against hers, soothing the soft contours before taking a slow, sweeping exploration. Teasing, tantalising in an evocative dance that came close to destroying her resolve.

The temptation to deepen the kiss was almost impossible to resist, but she managed it...just, and broke the contact. Only because he allowed her to.

'I want you to know I'm where I'm meant to be,' Mia said simply. 'With you.' She lifted a hand and placed gentle fingers over his mouth. 'Please. I need to say the words.'

She felt his lips caress her fingers, then still.

'You're my world. Everything.' Was that her voice? It sounded impossibly husky and drowning in emotion.

'I gift you my heart, unconditionally. My love.' There was nothing she could do about the well of moisture shimmering in her eyes.

'Thank you,' Nikolos said gently. 'It's a gift I'll treasure for the rest of my life.'

'There's just one more thing.' She moved quickly, taking him by surprise as she reversed their positions and straddled him. 'I get to have my turn.'

Mia lowered her head and brushed his mouth with her own. 'If you want to complain, do it now.'

He didn't utter a word.

CHAPTER ELEVEN

Two weeks later the Karedes family gathered together in the manicured gardens of Sofia Karedes' home.

It was a beautiful day for a wedding, the sun's late afternoon warmth reduced by a soft breeze whispering in from the harbour.

Mia wore an exquisitely crafted gown of ivory silk and lace with a lace-edged veil attached to an elegant headpiece. She carried a bouquet of pale peach-coloured roses, and wore an exquisite diamond pendant and earrings, a gift from the groom...who looked magnificent in Armani.

Alice stood in as the bride's attendant, with Cris acting as Nikolos' best man. Sofia and Angelena took pride of place as mother and grandmother of the groom. Matt was entrusted with the rings.

Costas stood on the sideline, a witness, observer, and Mia suspected, a bodyguard. He also acted as photographer, thus ensuring no unsolicited shots could be released to the media.

There was a sense of unreality as the celebrant intoned the words, and Mia's hand trembled a little as Nikolos slid the wide diamond-studded wedding ring onto her finger.

She was powerless to prevent the shimmer of moisture glistening in her eyes, and her lips parted in surprise as he leant forward and took possession of her mouth in a slow, evocative kiss that brought a soft tinge of pink to her cheeks.

'I don't think you were supposed to do that yet,' Mia murmured as he lifted his head.

'No?'

His voice held a latent sensuality that sent warmth flooding her body.

Then it was her turn to slip a gold band onto his finger, the celebrant concluded the ceremony, and Nikolos kissed the bride.

Affectionate hugs were exchanged and congratulations offered.

'I think I'm going to cry,' Alice warned quietly as the sisters embraced.

'Don't you dare.' Mia's voice shook a little. 'Think *happy*.'

'I *am* happy. You look absolutely stunning.'

'Somebody separate them,' Matt warned. 'We're talking *tears*.'

'Champagne and hors d'oeuvres are set up in the lounge,' Sofia announced, and placed a placating hand on Matt's shoulder. 'Happy tears are okay.'

Mia gently extricated herself and tucked her arm beneath Alice's elbow. 'Let's get you some champagne.'

Nikolos crossed to Matt's side as the party made their way into the house, and paused as the young boy slowed his steps to a halt.

'You'll take care of her, won't you?'

The young boy's earnestness was clearly visible, and Nikolos hunkered down so he was at eye level.

'Mia's special,' Matt continued doggedly.

'Very special,' Nikolos agreed gently, adding, 'I love her very much.'

Matt inclined his head. 'That's okay, then.'

Nikolos rose to his feet in one fluid movement and placed a casual arm round the young boy's shoulders. 'Let's go join the others, shall we?'

Mia saw man and boy enter the lounge, and watched as Nikolos crossed to her side. 'Man talk, huh?' she teased, and felt the breath hitch in her throat as he brushed gentle fingers across her cheek.

He had the ability to make her feel as if she were the only woman in his world. Love was something to be treasured, cherished...a gift beyond price.

'Have I told you how beautiful you are?'

She lifted her head and offered him a captivating smile. 'It's the dress,' she teased. 'All this finery gets to come off.'

His husky chuckle sent her pulse racing to a quickened beat as he leaned in close. 'Removing it will be my pleasure.'

Mia laid the palm of one hand against his cheek and offered him a wicked smile. 'Just be warned I get to return the favour.'

Dinner was served in the formal dining-room. A sumptuous meal with Costas in attendance.

'You'll do very well, child,' Angelena accorded as they sampled the dessert. 'It is a joy to see Nikolos so content.'

For all her blunt manner, the elderly matriarch possessed a soft heart, and Mia took hold of the arthritic hand and gave it a gentle squeeze. 'Thank you.'

There was a wedding cake, its intricate icing a work of art, and a small stack of miniature replicas for each guest, together with toasts to the bride and groom, more champagne, followed by coffee.

After which Nikolos caught hold of Mia's hand and indicated their intention to leave.

Not that they had far to go, for they'd elected to return to the Seaforth apartment. Christmas was only a week distant, and they wanted to spend it with family. Mid-January they'd fly to Athens and take a cruise round the Greek Islands.

'Happy, *agape mou*?' Nikolos queried as they entered the apartment.

'More than mere words can convey,' Mia said gently, and turned into his arms.

'I love you. More than life itself.'

The depth of emotion evident in his voice almost made her cry. 'You're everything to me,' she managed shakily as he gently freed the veil from her hair.

She stepped out of her shoes, and reached for the zip fastening of her gown.

There was a teasing quality evident as they began discarding each layer of clothes, pausing often for a lingering kiss as they slowly made their way towards the bedroom.

The gentle slide of a hand, the brush of his mouth, hers, in a tantalising exploration that fuelled the anticipation, the promise…heightening the sensuality and heating the passion until there was only shimmering, pulsating need.

As it would always be between them.

Love everlasting. Now and for ever.

EPILOGUE

Tyler Yannis Karedes made his entry into the world a week early, charming his adoring parents and gaining the adulation of his paternal grandmother and great-grandmother who unashamedly used every opportunity to visit, any excuse to watch over him.

His christening at three months of age was an intimate family event, with Alice, Cris and Matt chosen as godparents. Craig Mitchell was present as an invited guest.

Afterwards, Angelena, Sofia and Alice jostled affectionately for a turn to hold him, noting and commenting on each smile, every gurgle.

'He's enjoying every bit of it,' Mia said quietly as she surveyed the scene being played out in the spacious lounge of her home.

'Captivating his female audience,' Nikolos agreed as he drew her in against him.

'What he needs,' she declared, 'is a sibling to balance the scales of attention a little.'

'Mia—'

'After I sit my registration exams,' she mused thoughtfully, 'would be a good time, don't you think?'

Her delicate perfume teased his senses, and his arms tightened around her slender frame. She was so infinitely precious, so much a part of him. His life, his very soul.

'Not too soon?'

'You object?'

How could he? He'd adored every phase of her pregnancy...the wonder of their child growing in her womb. But nothing had prepared him for the joy of holding their newborn in his arms for the first time.

'My concern is for you.'

Mia's eyes began to mist. 'Maybe it'll be a girl this time.'

At the end of the year she'd gain her degree, and he had his eye on a new shopping complex where a pharmacy would be perfectly located. He already had a team of shop fitters awaiting her instructions, a dossier of CVs for a prospective manager and staff. It would allow her to run her own business, part-time, with the help of a part-time nanny. He intended the package to be his gift to her on their wedding anniversary.

'How soon before our guests leave, do you think?'

His husky voice sent a familiar flood of heat through her body, sensitising each nerve-end, every skin-cell until she ached for him and the sensual delight they shared.

'Another hour?' She sent him a teasing glance. 'Maybe two?'

'How do you feel about an early night?'

Her light laugh tugged at his heartstrings, and she took time to brush her lips against his in a fleeting kiss that didn't come close to easing the desire he felt for her.

It would take a lifetime, and then some. Love, true love, didn't die. It lived for ever, and beyond.

MILLS & BOON® PUBLISH EIGHT LARGE PRINT TITLES A MONTH. THESE ARE THE EIGHT TITLES FOR APRIL 2005

HIS PREGNANCY ULTIMATUM
Helen Bianchin

BEDDED BY THE BOSS
Miranda Lee

THE BRAZILIAN TYCOON'S MISTRESS
Fiona Hood-Stewart

CLAIMING HIS CHRISTMAS BRIDE
Carole Mortimer

TO WIN HIS HEART
Rebecca Winters

THE MONTE CARLO PROPOSAL
Lucy Gordon

THE LAST-MINUTE MARRIAGE
Marion Lennox

THE CATTLEMAN'S ENGLISH ROSE
Barbara Hannay

MILLS & BOON®

Live the emotion

0305 Rom LP

MILLS & BOON® PUBLISH EIGHT LARGE PRINT TITLES A MONTH. THESE ARE THE EIGHT TITLES FOR MAY 2005

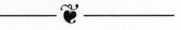

THE GREEK TYCOON'S CONVENIENT MISTRESS
Lynne Graham

HIS MARRIAGE ULTIMATUM
Helen Brooks

THE SHEIKH'S CONVENIENT BRIDE
Sandra Marton

THE MARCHESE'S LOVE-CHILD
Sara Craven

ASSIGNMENT: TWINS
Leigh Michaels

HER DESERT FAMILY
Barbara McMahon

HOW TO MARRY A BILLIONAIRE
Ally Blake

HER REAL-LIFE HERO
Trish Wylie

MILLS & BOON®

Live the emotion

0405 R